B

Caribbean Cri

"You'll find everything you need in the package," Q went on. "Since St. John is part of the United States, you won't need international cell phones—just bring your own. You have reservations at the Buccaneer's Lair Hotel, right in the heart of Cruz Bay. You can walk there from the ferry dock. It's where Esteban was staying when he disappeared."

"Don't worry, boss," Frank said to the screen, "we'll find this guy for you."

"That's about it, boys," Q finished. "Good luck, and happy traveling. If you get lucky and wind up the case quickly, you're, ahem, free to spend the rest of your week on the beach."

"Cool!" we both said at once.

"Oh—and this disc, as usual, will alter itself in five seconds . . . four . . . three . . . two . . . one . . ."

The screen switched to a pattern of onrushing stars, and the pounding reggae music of Insane Generation blasted out of the speakers.

UNDERCOVER BROTHERS™

#1 *Extreme Danger*
#2 *Running on Fumes*
#3 *Boardwalk Bust*
#4 *Thrill Ride*
#5 *Rocky Road*
#6 *Burned*
#7 *Operation: Survival*
#8 *Top Ten Ways to Die*
#9 *Martial Law*
#10 *Blown Away*
#11 *Hurricane Joe*
#12 *Trouble in Paradise*

Available from Simon & Schuster

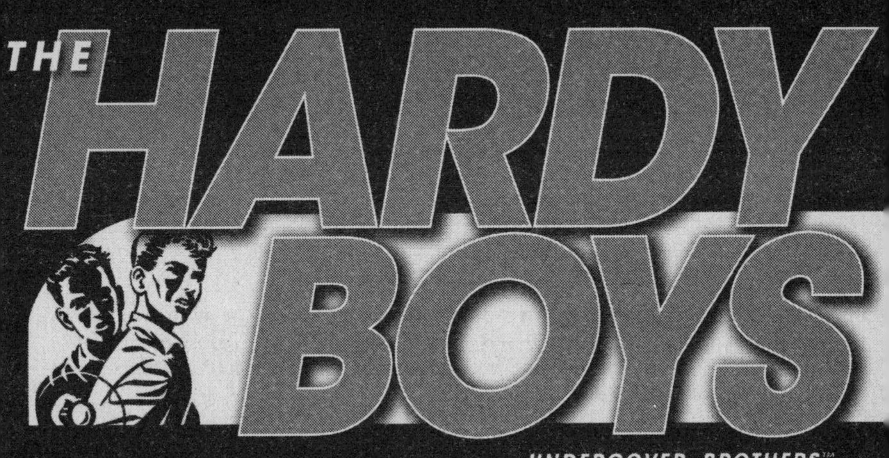

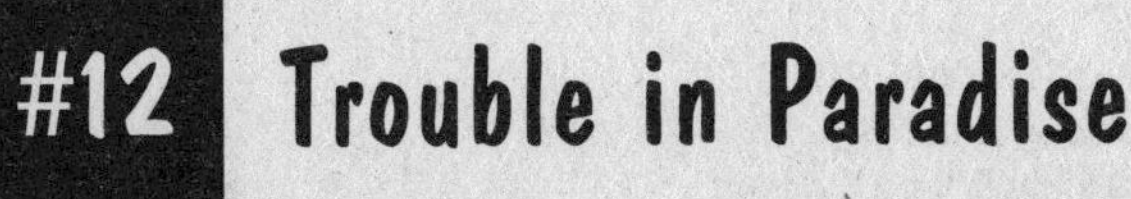

#12 Trouble in Paradise

FRANKLIN W. DIXON

Aladdin Paperbacks
New York London Toronto Sydney

First Aladdin Paperbacks edition October 2006

ALADDIN PAPERBACKS
An imprint of Simon & Schuster
Children's Publishing Division
1230 Avenue of the Americas
New York, NY 10020

Designed by Lisa Vega
The text of this book was set in Aldine 401BT.
Printed in the United States of America
10 9

Library of Congress Control Number: 2006926057

ISBN-13: 978-1-4169-1178-4
ISBN-10: 1-4169-1178-2
0312 OFF

TABLE OF CONTENTS

Trouble in Paradise

1.
Bats in the Belfry

I was hanging in midair, dangling from a rope. Flames roared up at me from below, singeing my brand-new, fur-lined winter boots.

Next to me, my brother Joe hung from an identical rope under a pair of huge, cast-iron church bells that rang out every time we squirmed. And we had to squirm a lot, to avoid getting burned by the intense heat coming up from below.

The smart thing to do in a situation like this is to climb up to the top of the belfry. But when your wrists are firmly tied to the rope, and they're holding up all your weight, that's easier said than done.

"Any ideas?" Joe asked me, raising his knees to his chest so his feet wouldn't get burned.

"I'm thinking, I'm thinking. Give me a second, will you?"

"I would, if we had a second to spare. And aren't you supposed to be the one with all the bright ideas?"

It's true. Between Joe and me, I'm the brother with the brainy reputation—although Joe's grades are mostly as good as mine. But I'm a year older, and Joe always looks to me for inspiration when we're in trouble.

But let me tell you, it's tough to come up with bright ideas when your foot's cooking!

"Start climbing!" I shouted over the noise of the bells, which was unbelievably loud. (No wonder the Hunchback of Notre Dame was deaf.)

"Right."

Using our knees to grab hold of the ropes, we moved like inchworms, lifting ourselves higher one handhold at a time.

"That's it!" I yelled. "Faster!"

Joe looked down, and I followed his gaze through the choking smoke. The floor of the belfry was a leaping, dancing inferno. The fire was climbing toward us a lot quicker than we could shimmy upward.

Still, it was the only way we could stay alive long enough for me to think of a better plan.

We kept it up, coughing and struggling to breathe. The ropes burned our hands and wrists as we climbed.

"Hot for December, huh?" Joe cracked between coughs.

He just can't help himself. It doesn't matter if we're facing imminent death—a good one-liner is too tempting for Joe to pass up.

"Ha, ha. I'm gonna die laughing," I said, coughing my guts up. "Keep climbing."

"Bro," Joe said, looking up at the bells, "we're gonna run out of room pretty soon."

He kept talking after that, but by now we were so close to the bells—only about twenty feet away—that every word was drowned out by clangs.

In about a minute, we'd be right alongside the bells, and they would start smashing into us. With the flames reaching higher along every wall, the metal of the bells would be red-hot, and we'd be . . .

Wait a second—that gave me an idea!

"Joe!"

He didn't hear me. I reached out with my foot and tapped him on the behind. He yelled something at me, looking annoyed—but at least he was looking at me now. If he couldn't hear, he could at least read my lips.

"I've got an idea!" I said, slowly mouthing the words so he could understand.

He nodded, showing he was with me.

"The bells will be hot. We can use the heat to burn through the ropes!"

He gave me a look like I was an idiot, then motioned downward slowly with his head and eyes. I got his drift: If the ropes burned through, we'd plummet to a fiery death.

"We've got to jump sideways, to the balcony, at exactly the right moment—just when the rope burns through!"

He looked at me blankly, shaking his head and shrugging.

"Watch me first!" I screamed.

That he got.

I shimmied up the last few feet, until I was just about inside the bell. Below me, my rope hung in a long loop, doubled up from the slack I'd created. The bottom of the loop was dangling dangerously close to the flames. If it caught fire, I'd be toast.

I reached over toward the bell as it came my way. The hot metal touched the rope, about a foot above my hands.

Immediately the rope started to smolder. I repeated the action on the bell's next swing—then again, and again, until the rope caught fire.

Now I started to swing myself toward the balcony and away, back and forth, trying to time my leap exactly right. Just as I felt the rope start to give way, I swung at the balcony, putting all my weight into it.

The rope snapped!

I landed in a heap—safe on the balcony, but with my wrists still tied to a foot of rope.

I looked across at Joe, who had already begun the same maneuver. I went around to the other side of the balcony, ready to give him as much of a hand as I could, what with both of them tied together.

Joe made his leap, but too soon—before his rope snapped—so I grabbed him with my bound hands and pulled, hard.

We toppled backward—and our combined weight snapped the rope, just as it was about to pull us back over the railing and into the inferno.

"*Ow*!" Joe yelled as he landed on top of me.

"Sorry for saving your life," I said sarcastically. "And it was *you* who landed on top. I'm the one who should be complaining."

"That's okay, bro—I forgive you. That was a pretty brilliant idea, by the way."

"Thanks."

"So now what?"

"Huh?"

"What are we supposed to do from here? Jump to the ground? It's, like, sixty feet down!"

I leaned out of the opening at the top of the bell tower. The full moon was out, and it made the snow-covered ground look blue—except for the reddish glow from the burning church.

I heard the sirens of the Bayport Fire Department in the distance. You'd think they would have been here by now, what with the bells ringing constantly. But then, I realized, it was Christmas Night. Every church bell in the world was ringing.

"Frank—the crèche!" Joe shouted, pointing to it with his bound hands.

The Christmas crèche featured a large manger on the church's front lawn. Its roof was covered with thick, soft hay.

A perfect landing spot.

"Maybe we should wait for the fire engines?" I suggested weakly.

Joe looked at the floor beneath us, which was already partly on fire. "I don't think so," he said.

"Okay," I said, swallowing hard. "After you."

"No," he said. "That crèche roof will never hold up twice. We jump together."

"All right."

We looked each other right in the eye. "One."

The balcony exploded in flames. We screamed "THREEEEEE!" and jumped.

Whumpfh!

A cloud of snow surrounded me. Everything hurt—but it was *good* pain, because feeling it meant I was still alive.

"Joe?"

"Ooohhh . . ."

"You okay?"

"I'm great. Just *great*."

"Hey, that was an awesome idea," I said.

"What was?"

"Jumping onto the roof of the crèche."

"Oh, that. . . . Was that really *my* idea? What was I thinking?"

Now I could see where we'd landed. The statue of the Virgin Mary looked down on me, smiling. Joe was covered by three plastic sheep.

Suddenly, the soot-covered faces of three Bayport firefighters appeared around the side of the wrecked manger.

"Somebody in there?" one of them asked.

"Just us sheep," Joe said.

"Hey, Joe, look," I said. "It's the three wise men."

"Merry Christmas, guys," Joe said. "Man, it's good to be alive."

They loaded us into an ambulance and took us to Bayport General Hospital for a quick patch-up.

A couple of hours later Chief Ezra Collig of the Bayport PD showed up, along with our dad, Fenton Hardy, who used to be a high-ranking policeman himself.

By the time they arrived, Joe and I were sitting in chairs, having our wrists bandaged by a couple of pretty nurses. The rope burns weren't too bad, considering.

"You boys could have been killed!" Dad said, frowning. "What were you doing up in that bell tower, anyway?"

"It wasn't like we had a choice," Joe said. "The Skulls tied us up and set the church on fire."

The Skulls are—make that *were*—a notorious biker gang. They had gotten it into their heads to expand their illegal operations into the Bayport area. That's when Joe and I were sent undercover to infiltrate their organization.

It all went really well, too—until Chet Morton, one of our buddies, accidentally gave away our true identities.

When they realized we were government agents, the Skulls got mad and decided to teach us a lesson. They tied us to those church bell ropes and set the steeple on fire.

"Can you identify the gang members who were involved?" Chief Collig asked.

"Sure thing," I said. "But you're going to have to find them first. Something tells me they won't be coming back to Bayport anytime soon."

"Thanks to you two," the chief said. "Fenton, you ought to be proud of these boys, not mad at them. They've done the town a great service, considering they're just a couple of amateurs."

Amateurs?

Ha. If he only knew.

Joe and I are special agents with ATAC (American Teens Against Crime), a secret organization our dad founded a couple of years back. We go on cases adults can't handle—say, infiltrating a teen biker gang like the Skulls.

"You know, Fenton," Chief Collig went on, "these boys deserve a nice big Christmas present."

"How about a vacation?" Joe piped up, giving Dad an innocent smile.

A vacation?

"Joe, you're just *full* of good ideas tonight," I said. "I couldn't agree more."

2.
Surprise Package

Dad drove us home from the hospital. He was in a really bad mood—not a good sign on Christmas. I could tell something was eating at him.

"What's the matter, Dad?" I asked.

He frowned. "In my day, we didn't have to go risking our lives all the time just to catch the bad guys."

"With all due respect, Dad," I said, "in your day, they matched fingerprints by hand, and there was no such thing as DNA evidence."

Frank leaned forward from the backseat. "Dad, it's not like we try to get ourselves in trouble. It just *happens*."

"I'd just hate to see you boys get hurt," he said, his jaw tight.

"Don't worry, Dad," I said, putting a hand on his shoulder. "We can take care of ourselves. After all, we learned from the best there is."

"Oh, it's not *me* who's worried," he said (not that we believed him). "It's your mother and your Aunt Trudy. I phoned to let them know why you didn't show up for Christmas dinner. They're both frantic."

"You didn't tell them the *whole story*, did you?" Frank asked.

Dad frowned again. "You know I didn't."

See, Mom and Aunt Trudy don't know a thing about ATAC. They think our detective work is strictly amateur, and they keep advising us not to take any foolish chances.

So you can imagine the fuss they made when Frank and I showed up that night with our wrists bandaged and our eyebrows singed.

"What in the world have you boys been up to this time?" Aunt Trudy demanded. Meanwhile, Mom fell apart in tears and started hugging and kissing us both.

"We got caught in a fire over at the church," Frank said.

"Just trying to be good Samaritans," I explained, hoping that would be enough of an explanation for them.

"Are you badly hurt?" Mom asked, looking over our bandages.

"It's nothing, Mom," I assured her. "Just minor burns. We'll be fine in a couple of days. Don't worry, please."

"Awwkk! Medic! Medic!"

This comment came from Playback, our pet parrot—who was perched, as usual, on Aunt Trudy's shoulder.

"Really, we're fine," Frank said. "Right, Dad?"

"You would have been proud of them, Laura," Dad said. "They're a couple of brave boys."

"Being brave is fine," Mom said, "but it doesn't mean you have to put yourselves in harm's way."

Nobody argued with her. What was the point? She was never going to stop worrying about us, and we were never going to stop fighting crime.

We ate dinner, and Mom's turkey never tasted better. But Frank and I were both about to conk out. Hanging by your wrists and breathing smoke is *tiring*!

Frank let out a big yawn. "Boy, I'm beat."

"Me too," I said.

"Wouldn't you boys like something else to eat before you head up to bed?" Mom asked. "Some dessert? I have plum pudding."

"No thanks, Mom, I'm stuffed," I said.

"I need to crash," Frank said.

"Ditto," I said.

"Awwkk! Wanna cracker?"

"Thanks, Playback," I said. "Maybe some other time."

"Wanna cookie?"

"Hush now," Trudy told him.

And he did. Playback listens to her, and to nobody else.

The next morning Frank and I both slept late. By the time we came down to breakfast, Dad had already left for his office. (He's supposedly retired, but he still works pretty hard, making sure everything's running smoothly with ATAC.)

"My, my," Mom said, smiling. "I thought you boys were going to sleep the whole day away."

"It's so quiet," Frank said. "Where are Aunt Trudy and Playback?"

"She's out in the driveway, changing the oil in her car. Playback's with her, naturally."

(That parrot follows her everywhere. He must think he's her child or something. She certainly *treats* him that way, even if they have a love/hate relationship.)

"The mailman's already been here," Mom told us. She dropped a fat envelope on the table. "This came for you, boys. Looks like junk mail, but I didn't want to throw it out before you saw it."

It did look like a piece of junk mail. But on the envelope, it said: YOU HAVE WON A FREE VACATION!

The magic words! I tore open the envelope before Frank could make a grab for it.

"'Congratulations, Frank and Joe Hardy!'" I read out loud. "'You have been chosen to enjoy a free vacation in that American Paradise—the U.S. Virgin Islands!'"

"Yeah, like I believe that," Frank said.

I ignored him. "It sounds perfect! Can't you just picture us, partying New Year's Eve away on the beach? And just think—it wouldn't cost Mom and Dad a penny!"

It was only December, but we'd already had enough snow for a whole winter. We'd been skiing and snowboarding until we were sick of it. And now, after our recent brush with death, we *needed* to rest our tired, sore bodies on a tropical beach. *Needed* it. *Bad!*

"Don't get too excited," Frank said. "These junk mail offers are usually scams. They try to get you to buy worthless land, or time-shares, or whatever. You go on this supposedly free vacation, and then they ruin it for you by giving you the hard-sell treatment, nagging and nagging you until you hand over your money."

"Okay, but then why send it to *us*? Why not to Mom and Dad? I mean, they're the ones with enough money to buy property, not us."

Frank's face went blank. "You're right, Joe—there's something funny about this 'free vacation.' Someone must have made a mistake. Throw it out."

"Oh, no—we're not turning this down, dude. A vacation's a vacation!" I grabbed the letter and the pictures of perfect Caribbean beaches that came with it. "Seems like a good offer to me. I say we go!"

At the bottom of the letter, it said, "To claim your free vacation, call this toll-free number within twenty-four hours!" I went over to the counter, picked up the cordless phone, and started punching in the numbers.

But I stopped before I finished—because I realized something. The number I was dialing was 1-800-CALL-ATAC!

"Frank," I said, "We've *got* to check this out."

"Aw, forget it, will you? Like I said, it's just a piece of junk—throw it out. We don't want any worthless property."

I checked to see whether Mom was listening.

She was busy going through some papers from work (she's Bayport's head librarian).

"Frank. Listen to me," I said softly. *"I think we should check this out.* Okay?" I showed him the 800 number.

"Ohhh. Yeah, Joe. Good idea. Let's call them."

"How 'bout we go outside and see what Aunt Trudy's up to?" I suggested, nodding toward Mom.

We went outside with the phone and the letter.

Sure enough, Aunt Trudy was underneath her forest green VW Beetle, working away. Only her legs showed, and she was wearing some funny orthopedic shoes. Playback was perched on the hood of the car, whistling a part of the theme song to that old show *Gilligan's Island*. Too much TV.

Frank and I headed for the backyard. Right now we wanted privacy, not TV music. We sat down on the bench by our back fence.

"I suppose it could be just a coincidence," Frank said.

"Yeah? What are the odds?" I said, punching in the number.

"Prize redemption center," a female voice chirped.

"Hi," I said. "I'm calling about the, um, free vacation?"

"What's the code number on your certificate?" she asked.

I checked, then read it out to her. "F5XS43R."

There was a short pause. "For verification, what is the street number of your residence?"

"Four five zero."

Another short pause. "And could you verify your father's name?"

"Fenton Hardy," I said. Then, for good measure, I added, "I'm Joe."

"Wonderful. Mr. Hardy, congratulations. You and your brother will be receiving a free vacation in the American Paradise, the U.S. Virgin Islands, all expenses paid."

"Uh, just a second," I stopped her. "What's the story here?"

"Excuse me?"

"You know—what's up?"

She giggled. "There's nothing to buy, sir, if that's what you mean. This is an entirely free vacation."

I got it now—of course, she couldn't talk about ATAC stuff over the phone.

"You'll be receiving all the necessary materials by express delivery, Mr. Hardy."

"I see. And when will that be?"

"Let me check. . . . The package should be arriving . . . in approximately ten seconds."

"Huh?"

The phone went dead. At the same time, I heard

the rumble of a truck coming down the street. Getting up, I went around the side of the house, with Frank right behind me.

Sure enough, there was an Express Post truck out front!

Aunt Trudy was already wiping engine oil off her hands with a rag and demanding that the deliveryman give the package to her.

"Sorry, ma'am," he was saying. "This can only be delivered in person to either Frank or Joe Hardy."

"Well!" said Aunt Trudy, clearly peeved.

Playback flew to Trudy's shoulder and spread his wings wide, trying to scare the poor deliveryman. "Aawwk! Run him through! Avast, me hearties!"

"Has that thing had its shots?" he asked nervously.

"'That thing' is healthier than you are!" Aunt Trudy snapped.

"Here, I'll sign for that," I said, stepping forward.

"You Frank Hardy?"

"Joe."

"All right, that'll do." He gave me his clipboard to sign.

"Thanks."

He gave Trudy and Playback a look and shook

his head. "Boy. Some people." Then he got back into his truck and drove away.

"Some people indeed!" Trudy said, still angry. "I've never met anyone so rude in my entire life!"

She stared down at the package in my hand. She was obviously waiting for me to open it in front of her.

No way was I going to do that. I knew by now what was inside—our next case!

That's one thing about the great organization we work for—they give us our assignments in the most surprising ways. It's fun, but sometimes it's a pain—like *now*.

"Um, Joe," Frank said, coming to my rescue, "that must be the 'Grow Your Own Scorpion' science kit that Chet wanted us to order for him."

"The *what*?" Aunt Trudy screamed. "Get that thing out of here! And don't you dare bring it in the house, either!"

I bit my lip, trying hard to keep a straight face.

But if Aunt Trudy wasn't going to let us take it inside, how were we going to open the box in peace?

Luckily, when Aunt Trudy screamed, Playback got spooked. He took off into the air and landed in the high branches of a nearby oak tree. He sat there, screeching for all he was worth, imitating

Aunt Trudy. "Get that thing out of here! Aaawwk!"

Trudy forgot all about the box. "Help! Somebody call the fire department!" she yelled.

Mom came running out the front door. "Trudy, whatever's the matter?" she asked.

Trudy pointed upward, her lips trembling.

"Aawwk! Call the fire department! Call the fire department!" Playback screamed, mocking her.

"Now, Trudy," Mom said, putting a soothing hand on our aunt's shoulder. "Playback's a bird. He can fly. I'm sure he'll come down when he's ready. We feed him, after all. Steady food source."

While Trudy slowly calmed down, Frank and I slipped back into the house with our box.

We got upstairs to Frank's room and locked the door behind us. Then we emptied the package's contents onto the bed.

"Hmmm . . . ," Frank said. "Airline tickets to the U.S. Virgin Islands. Hey, they weren't kidding!"

"You see?" I said, "sometimes junk mail really is worth reading."

"And here we have a pair of credit cards. . . . wow—a one-thousand-dollar credit line . . ."

"Excellent! Party time!" I flopped back onto Frank's bed. "This is going to be a really fun time, I can tell."

"And a wad of cash . . ."

"Keep going."

"Prepaid scooter rental . . ."

"Awesome."

"Police report . . ."

"Aw, you had to go and ruin it." I made a face and covered my head with Frank's pillow.

"Cut it out, Joe. You know you wouldn't enjoy a vacation unless there was some crime fighting attached to it."

The pillow came off my head. "You're right. What was I thinking? Police report? Fantastic! What else have we got?"

"Just this DVD. Shall I?"

"Go ahead."

He popped it into the DVD player, and I sat up in bed to watch.

The kindly, round face of Q, one of the intel guys at ATAC, came onto the screen. *Hello, boys*, he said, giving us a smile. *Welcome to your next case. I think you're going to like this one.*

His image faded, replaced by an aerial view of the most beautiful tropical island you'd ever want to see.

This is St. John, Q's voice went on. *It's part of the U.S. Virgin Islands. It's only a short ferry ride from busy St. Thomas, but St. John is very different. Most of it is permanently preserved as a national park. The island has only about five thousand permanent residents, and most of them live in the main town, Cruz Bay. There's only one big luxury hotel—the famous Caneel Bay Resort. You'll be staying in more humble digs, of course. And we're not sending you to St. John just for a vacation, I'm afraid. It seems there's trouble in paradise.*

The screen changed to a picture of a young guy, maybe a little older than me and Frank. He had dark hair, dark eyes, a deep tan, and a bright, perfect smile.

This is Esteban Calderon. He is a well-known member of the international jet set. More importantly, he is the son of Don Ricardo Calderon, the United Nations ambassador from Santa Cruz. Don Ricardo is a major power at the World Bank.

Esteban was last seen club-hopping in Cruz Bay on the night of December eighteenth. The following afternoon, his rented Jeep was found abandoned, near the ruins of an old sugar mill on the north coast of the island, at Leinster Bay. Don Ricardo seems to think his son has been kidnapped—but it's been a week, and there's been no ransom note.

"Okay," Frank said to the screen, "but why send *us*?"

You're probably wondering why I've chosen to send you boys, Q said, right on cue (so to speak). *It seems Don Ricardo is kicking up quite a fuss. Diplomatically, this is a delicate matter. The local police and the FBI spent a couple of days looking into it, but then we got orders from higher up to back off. It seems the territorial government complained.*

We can understand why they don't want a bunch of uniformed police or military down there, scaring off all the tourists. But the United States can't afford to upset the World Bank, or the people of Santa Cruz—one of our major oil suppliers. We need to solve this case. That's where you boys come in.

Esteban is twenty-one years old. As teens, you may be able to go unnoticed in places where adult law enforcement can't.

"Like all-night reggae beach parties?" I said. "Count us in!"

You'll find everything you need in the package, Q went on. *Since St. John is part of the United States, you won't need international cell phones—just bring your own. You have reservations at the Buccaneer's Lair Hotel, right in the heart of Cruz Bay. You can walk there from the ferry dock. It's where Esteban was staying when he disappeared.*

"Don't worry, boss," Frank said to the screen, "we'll find this guy for you."

That's about it, boys, Q finished. *Good luck, and happy traveling. If you get lucky and wind up the case quickly, you're, ahem, free to spend the rest of your week on the beach.*

"Cool!" we both said at once.

Oh—and this disc, as usual, will alter itself in five seconds . . . four . . . three . . . two . . . one . . .

The screen switched to a pattern of onrushing stars, and the pounding reggae music of Insane Generation blasted out of the speakers.

3.
Welcome to Paradise

"You don't mean to say you're really planning to *go*?" Aunt Trudy's face was a picture of horror. Perched on her shoulder, Playback hopped up and down nervously.

"Sure we are!" Joe said. "Why not? It's a holiday week. There's no school. And besides, it's not every day you win something *really big*!"

"Oh, that's a bunch of hooey," she shot back.

"Hooey! Hooey!" Playback echoed, flapping his wings for emphasis.

"Don't you boys know that all these so-called free vacations are really scams? You'll get down there and find out your hotel's booked solid—or worse, that it doesn't even exist. And you think it's all going to be free? Mark my words, you'll end up having to pay top dollar for everything!"

You know, I could have sworn Aunt Trudy was jealous. Luckily, Mom was there to calm her down.

"Now, Trudy," she said, in that gentle voice of hers, "I'm sure the boys will be fine. Fenton checked up on the company running the contest, and he seems satisfied they're legitimate."

"Humph," Trudy replied. "You'll see, Laura—they'll wind up getting pressured to buy some falling-apart condo in the middle of a swamp."

"We've gotta go upstairs and pack now," I said, giving Aunt Trudy a kiss on the forehead. "Don't worry, Aunt T—we'll be fine, you'll see. We'll bring you back a souvenir."

"If you were my children, I wouldn't spoil you like this," she grumbled. "You boys had better stay out of trouble down there, you hear?"

"We promise," Joe said quickly. "Right, Frank?"

"Sure. Come on, Joe, let's get busy."

We climbed the stairs, with Playback shouting, "Hooey! Hooey!" behind us.

The flight to St. Thomas on December 27th was long, but the plane had video game screens for every seat, so Joe was totally happy.

Me, I kept busy reading up on St. John. I always like to know something about a place before I go there for the first time.

"Listen to this, Joe," I said. "St. John was a favorite hideout of pirates in the late 1500s and 1600s. Sir Francis Drake's fleet hid at Coral Bay and Leinster Bay, waiting for Spanish treasure ships to come by so they could plunder them. That means the Virgin Islands have some of the best wreck diving in the world—and there's supposed to be lots of sunken treasure, too! Hey, Joe, are you listening?"

He was glued to the video screen.

"Yaa! Take that, freakazoid!" He pressed a button, blasting several space monsters at once. Then he paused his game. "Hmm? Did you say something, Frank?"

"Never mind," I said. "Have fun."

"Oh. Okay." He shrugged and went back to his virtual world.

I could relate. After fighting the Skulls and nearly getting burnt to a crisp—in a *church*, on *Christmas*, no less—fighting freakazoids must have felt like a piece of cake!

I kept reading. Two-thirds of St. John's land had been bought up by this super-rich guy, Laurance Rockefeller, and given to the National Park Service so it could be preserved forever.

"One of the best hikes in the national park is the Reef Bay Trail," my guidebook said. "You start at the top of a mountain and walk downhill all day, past waterfalls and exotic jungle terrain. The trail ends at an isolated beach, where there's an old abandoned sugar mill from colonial days. There, a boat picks you up and takes you back to town."

I circled the page—maybe Joe and I could tear ourselves away from our case long enough to take a little hike.

We landed on St. Thomas, retrieved our bags, and went outside to find a taxi. The heat hit us like a slap in the face.

"Whoa!" Joe said. "Wait a second."

He took off his sweatshirt and stuffed it in his backpack. Then we hailed a cab for the ride to the St. John ferry.

"How far is it?" Joe asked the cabbie.

"All the way across the island, mon."

Our cabbie gave us a gold-toothed smile from behind his mirrored shades and said, "No worries, mon. We gonna get there plenty time. Meanwhile, you sit back and enjoy the view, and let Beanie Man do the drivin'."

We followed his advice, basking in the warm Caribbean breeze, perfumed by tropical flowers and diesel exhaust. (Hey, at least it was warm!)

We passed through Charlotte Amalie, the busy, traffic-choked capital of the U.S. Virgin Islands, with its huge cruise ship docks, old colonial-era houses, and tiny, narrow streets packed with jewelry shops.

"That be all pirate gold them sellin', mon," Beanie Man said, flashing those gold teeth and laughing at his own joke.

Our cab wound back and forth up hairpin turns, climbing the island's volcanic hills until we got to the top of a ridge. From there, we got our first look eastward at St. John across the strait.

Like St. Thomas, it was hilly and forested. *Unlike* St. Thomas, there were very few houses dotting the hillsides.

We said good-bye to our smiling cabbie at the ferry dock, making sure to give him a hefty tip for getting us there safely—no easy job when you're racing down narrow roads dodging cars, scooters, goats, and tourists.

Joe and I lugged our bags onto the ferry, found a couple of lounge chairs, and settled in for a late afternoon mini-cruise.

Half an hour later, we pulled into the dock at Cruz Bay, St. John. This would be our home for the next week. Because even if we found Esteban Calderon that very night, we had no intention of heading back north to the cold and snow. Not until we had to for school, anyway—and that wasn't till after New Year's Day.

"Okay," Joe said as we stepped off the ramp and onto the dock. "Where to now?"

"To the Buccaneer's Lair," I said. "It's on Lagoon Road. See any signs?"

We looked around. Cruz Bay was a beautiful place with a slow, small-town feel. There was a palm-shaded town park in front of us. Across the harbor to our left was the National Park headquarters.

To our right was a small outdoor mini-mall. "Looks like a good place to get directions," I said.

"And maybe a bite to eat," Joe said, hoisting his backpack. "I'm starving. Let's go."

We headed over there, passing stalls that sold coral jewelry, coconut wall hangings, and other trinkets to the tourists.

I noticed that we were the only ones in jeans and sneakers. Everyone else seemed to be wearing shorts or bathing suits, with sandals on their feet if they weren't going barefoot.

"Man," Joe said, "I think I'm gonna like it here. No, check that—I *know* I'm gonna like it here."

His head swiveled 180 degrees as a couple of girls in bikinis walked by, sipping smoothies.

"Mmmm," I said, "I could really use one of those."

"Just one?" Joe asked, smiling.

"I meant the smoothies."

I hate it when Joe rubs it in about me and girls. He *knows* I'm totally shy around them. My stomach gets all jumpy and I always say or do something stupid.

Meanwhile, he's got all these smooth moves. It really kills me.

"Okay, then." Joe sat down at an outdoor table by Jumpin' Jake's Smoothie Stand.

"Don't you want to check in to our hotel first?" I asked him.

"You said you were thirsty," he said. "And I'm starving. The hotel can wait."

I gave up. "I'll go get the smoothies," I said. "What flavor do you want?"

"How about piña colada?"

"Okay."

"Get me a cheeseburger and some fries, too, okay?"

That stopped me. "What am I, the waiter? Get it yourself, bro. I'm not standing on two lines while you sit here loafing."

"Yeah, but we'll lose our table if we both get up."

I looked around. There had to be half a dozen empty tables. It was about five in the afternoon, and most people were probably back in their rooms, getting ready for dinner.

"I think our table will still be here," I said.

I got on line and ordered two smoothies from the guy behind the counter. I figured he was Jumpin' Jake because the name seemed to fit. He had mirrored shades on and a big green leather cap. He looked rockin'.

"Excuse me," I said, while he was running the blender. "I'm looking for the Buccaneer's Lair. Can you tell me where it is?"

He stopped blending and gave me a slow once-over. Something about the way he was eyeing me gave me the creeps.

"Yeah, mon," he said. "It's just across the park, and two blocks up the hill. You can't miss it."

He gave me the smoothies and my change. Just as I was leaving, he leaned over the counter toward me and said, "Sure you want to stay there?"

"Huh? Why wouldn't I?"

"People been disappearing from there, mon."

"Really? Tell me more."

One thing I've learned—never let an opportunity go by.

He shrugged. "Nothing much to tell. But I've got a hotel just up the road—much nicer, and just as cheap."

SUSPECT PROFILE

Name: Jumpin' Jake

Hometown: Charlotte Amalie, St. Thomas, U.S.V.I.

Physical description: Age 48, 6', 230 lbs., dark complexion, hair stuffed under big cap, graying hair, leering dark eyes.

Occupation: Smoothie stand owner, hotel owner, and who knows what else?

Background: Grew up poor on St. Thomas. Somehow made enough money to buy his hotel and the smoothie stand. No one knows how he got the money, and he's not telling.

Suspicious behavior: Threatening Frank? Hard to tell.

Suspected of: Involvement with Esteban Calderon's disappearance.

Motive: Ransom?

"Uh, thanks, but we're all set."

"Hmm. As you like, mon. Welcome to the island. I just hope you don't be the next one gone."

"Uh . . . thanks."

Was he warning me? Or was he just angry that I didn't switch to his hotel?

I took the drinks, turned around, and nearly barreled into the girl behind me on line. She had long, wavy red hair and huge green eyes that sparkled like jewels.

"Whoa! Sorry!" I said, feeling my face go red.

"That's okay." She gave me a big, perfect, dimpled smile, and I'm sure my face got even redder. "I'm fine."

"You sure? I didn't spill anything on you?"

She laughed—a musical laugh that made me feel dizzy for a second. "I heard you say you were looking for the Buccaneer's Lair?"

"Uh-huh." (What a stupid thing to say! "Uh-huh." Why couldn't I have thought of some cool comeback? I am such a dork!)

"I work there, actually," she said. "I could walk you over if you like."

Would I like? Yes, I would like!

But I couldn't just leave Joe hanging. "Um, I've gotta wait for my brother," I said, sounding totally lame, I'm sure.

"Oh. Okay. Well, see you when you get there!" She gave me another dazzling smile. "Just ask for Jenna."

"Jenna," I repeated, like a dummy.

"What's your name?" she asked.

What *was* my name?

"Um . . . Frank! Yeah, that's it, um, Frank."

"Nice to meet you, 'UmFrank.'" She offered me her hand. It was tan, smooth, and had lots of rings on it.

"You too," I said, shaking it gently, like it was made of glass. "See you." She sashayed away.

I turned back to the table, defeated—and there was Joe, grinning at me.

"You dog, you!" he said. "I turn around for one minute, and you're putting the moves on the finest girl on the whole island."

"Cut it out," I told him. "I'm not in the mood for your warped sense of humor."

"Ex-cuuuse me," Joe said, pushing a hamburger platter across the table to me. "Here. Eat. Drink. Later you'll be merry."

The Buccaneer's Lair had a wooden sign hanging over the front door. It swayed gently in the breeze, along with the palm trees that shaded the entrance.

"Sweet," Joe said.

"I can't wait to crash and take a good nap."

"What? Did you just say 'nap'? Hey, bro, we're going out dancing tonight!"

"Dancing? No way."

"*Way*. Have you forgotten we're on a case?"

"Of course I haven't forgotten. So?"

"So, I figure we've got to talk to as many people as possible."

"And therefore?"

"And therefore, we should start with the finest young ladies we can find—after all, if this guy Esteban is all he's cracked up to be, they're the ones he was probably talking to the most."

He had a point.

"In fact," Joe went on, "I'd say that since he was staying at this hotel, he must have noticed that extremely fine young lady you were talking to before. Right?"

"You know, Joe, I've got to hand it to you. Every once in a while, you come up with an idea that doesn't stink."

"Ahhh," he said, smiling. "He admits it! Somebody get it down on paper, before he denies he ever said it!"

"Come on," I said, shaking my head and laughing, "let's go inside."

We walked past the uncomfortably real-looking statue of a one-eyed pirate, complete with saber, and entered the hotel lobby. In the rear was a bar and restaurant, with reggae music booming out of the speakers.

Lo and behold, there was Jenna behind the reception desk, waiting to check us in.

Joe didn't waste any time. "Hello, there, young lady," he said, laying on the charm—a little thickly, I thought.

Jenna looked at me. "This is your brother?"

"Uh, yeah," I said, shrugging my shoulders. "Joe, Jenna. Jenna, Joe."

She held out her heavily ringed hand to him. Instead of shaking it, he took it and kissed it.

Jenna looked at me again, as if to ask, *Is he mental?*

I shrugged again, as if to answer, *Joe's Joe. Nothing I can do about it.*

"I just need to run your credit cards and get you to sign," she said, taking back her hand. "Here are the keys to your room—it's number eight, on the top floor. You're free to use the hot tub on the roof."

"Cool," I said.

"Maybe you'd like to join us there later?" Joe asked her.

She let out a little laugh. "We'll see."

Meaning, *Don't hold your breath.*

Joe took the keys—the old-fashioned skeleton type. "All righty, then," he said. "Come on, Frank."

I followed him down the hall, giving Jenna a last little wave. She returned it with a smile and a wink.

Whoa.

"Dude," I told Joe when we were out of earshot. "You were way out of control there."

Joe laughed and slapped me on the back. "No worries, mon," he said, in a terrible try at Beanie Man's accent. "Don't worry, be happy."

"Yeah, right."

"It's all good," he said, opening the door to our room. "Trust me, brother—that girl *likes* you."

"Yeah. As if."

"You can believe it or not, dude, but I'll tell you one thing—we're starting our investigation with her. And *you're* the one who's going to do the investigating."

JOE

Joe here.

My brother can be such a doofus. He meets this gorgeous girl, who happens to be a perfect way into the investigation, and he just wants to stay in our room and sleep?

I'm a big fan of sleep, don't get me wrong—but

not at night! The time for sleep is the morning, after a long night of having fun.

He can stay here—but I'm heading out.

Gotta start investigating, mon!

Catch you later.

4.

The Buccaneer's Lair

I thought about Joe's words as I lay on my bed in the hotel room, letting the cool breeze from the ceiling fan blow over me. Outside, the sun was going down over St. Thomas, and the sea was glittering red, purple, and gold.

Now that I'd showered and changed, I suddenly wasn't so tired anymore. I could hear the sounds of reggae bands warming up for the evening's entertainment—they must have been coming from downtown.

Behind me, I heard the shower going—Joe taking his turn, washing off the dirt of the trip—and wondered just what exactly we were getting ourselves into.

We'd been badly bruised and battered, not to

mention burned, on our last case. It had only been two days since we'd wound it up, with the entire Skull leadership in police custody.

We badly needed a week off to recover before school started. And we were in the perfect place to do it. There was just one problem. . . .

We had a mission. Esteban Calderon had disappeared, in a place where it was very hard to disappear—namely, an island that was only nine miles long and five miles wide. There was nowhere to hide, unless he'd drowned and been washed out to sea.

Not a pretty thought. But I had to believe that if the son of a prominent international diplomat had really been kidnapped, it had to have been a professional job. And surely any professional kidnapper worth his salt would have whisked him off this tiny island by now.

So I didn't really expect to find Esteban here on St. John. What I *did* hope we'd find was a trail that would lead us to him, wherever he'd been taken.

According to the police records in the packet we'd received, Esteban had already been gone for nine days.

And in all that time, there'd been no ransom note?

Strange.

See, if you kidnap someone who's worth a lot of ransom money, you want to get that money, get the victim off your hands (one way or another), and get out of town—*as soon as possible.*

So why wasn't there a note, after nine long days?

The only thing I could think of was that something *really bad* had happened to Esteban.

Joe came out of the shower, toweling himself off. "Aw, man, that was great," he said. "You ready to go out and par-tay?"

"You go," I told him.

"What, are you beat already?" he said, flicking his towel at me.

"Ow! Cut that out!"

He laughed. "Seriously, bro, you're not gonna punk out on me tonight, are you?"

"I thought I'd stay around here," I said. "Maybe ask around about Esteban. Maybe get a look at the room he stayed in . . ."

"Maybe get closer to that girl Jenna," Joe said. "Hunh? Hunh? I *knew* it. Frank's got a crush!"

"Cut it out, will you?" I said. "I'm in no mood for fooling around."

"Okay," he said, backing off. "Let's talk about the alleged kidnap victim."

"Alleged?"

"I was thinking about it—this Esteban guy probably just felt like disappearing for a while. You know, getting away from it all, being totally alone, without paparazzi and stuff."

Hmmm. I hadn't thought of that possibility, but maybe Joe was right.

"According to the police report, Esteban's dad told them his son would never go anywhere without letting his parents know."

"On the other hand, as we all know, some parents haven't got a clue what their kids are up to."

"Aw, come on, Frank. It's been a long day—let's clear our heads for a couple of hours. Aren't you even coming out for dinner?"

I shook my head. "Thanks, but that burger did me in. It was huge. I'll just do my investigating right here at the hotel."

"You disappoint me, bro. Man, you're getting old fast."

Joe put some aftershave on and stuck his wallet and cell phone in his pocket. "Well, I'll call you in a while and see if you've changed your mind."

"Cool," I said, flicking my phone open and turning it on.

"If you're . . . ahem . . . with Jenna, you don't have to pick up the phone. I'll understand."

He went out the door, narrowly avoiding the pillow I threw at his head.

Joe can be so annoying sometimes!

I went downstairs and into the bar. Jenna was nowhere in sight—but that was fine with me.

The bartender was a big guy who looked like he pumped iron all day long. In fact, he looked more like a bouncer, what with his buzz cut and his thick, dark eyebrows. "What'll it be?" he asked me. "You got ID?"

"Oh, I'm not twenty-one," I said. "I'll just have an iced tea."

"We don't have iced tea," he said. "This is a bar, not a restaurant."

"Well," I said, "what have you got, then?"

"Club soda, cranberry juice, lemonade . . ."

"I'll have a lemonade."

He seemed to relax a little. "Sure thing," he said, and went to get it.

I looked around the room. There were tourists sitting at little tables, looking relaxed and happy. The reggae music that had been blasting from the speakers before was silent now—probably because the live music was going to start soon. I could see a pair of guys with dreadlocks hauling a steel drum in through the service door at the back of the bar.

"Here you go," the bartender said, bringing me my drink. "Put it on your room tab?"

"Uh, yeah—number eight," I said. "Hey . . . isn't this the hotel where that missing guy was staying?"

Suddenly, it was like I'd dropped a bomb. The bartender stared down at me. His dark eyebrows gathered together like a pair of storm clouds.

One by one, every table in the room fell silent. I could feel everyone's eyes on me.

"What are you, a reporter or something?" the bartender asked, his hands curling slowly into fists.

"Me? No, man. I'm not old enough. Don't you have to be twenty-one or something?" I laughed—too loudly. Nobody joined in.

"We don't talk about that," the bartender said. "People here are trying to have a good time, y'know?"

I noticed the muscles bulging out of his sleeves and wondered again if he doubled as the bouncer.

I sipped my lemonade, which was colored bright yellow—probably artificial coloring. "Mmmm . . . good," I said, wincing because the lemonade was so sour. "No, I was just asking because, you know, it was in the papers and stuff."

"Which papers?"

"Um, back home . . . in Bayport."

"Bayport!"

SUSPECT PROFILE

Name: The Bartender

Hometown: Los Angeles, CA

Physical description: Age 24, 6' 3", 210 lbs., suntanned, blue eyes, buzz cut, thick dark eyebrows that come together when he gets mad.

Occupation: Bartender, maybe also bouncer

Background: Former valley boy and gym rat who found the Caribbean and never left. Dresses well and never misses an opportunity.

Suspicious behavior: Threatening Frank, possibly sneaking into Frank and Joe's room to search their stuff?

Suspected of: Trying to hide the truth about Esteban Calderon's disappearance.

Motive: Fear of exposure?

"Yeah, apparently his dad is some big pooh-bah?"

"Look, I don't know where Bayport is, but here, we don't mess in other people's business," he said, leaning over toward me and cracking his knuckles.

"No. 'Course not. Me neither." I picked up my

drink and stood up. "'Scuse me." I tried to look casual as I sauntered away from him, heading out of the bar to the outdoor deck lounge.

It was a calm, beautiful night, and the stars were coming out in bunches. The town of Cruz Bay sprawled out below us, its lights twinkling. Without the bartender breathing down my neck and all the customers staring at me, I could finally breathe again.

Of course, I understood why he didn't want to talk about the kidnapping. It had to be bad for the Buccaneer's Lair's business. But I needed to ask questions if I ever expected to find Esteban Calderon.

I thought about the picture of him in the packet we'd gotten. A young, handsome guy; a real jet-setter . . .

Joe was right: If anyone around this small island remembered him, it would be the women—especially the young, good-looking ones.

I was staring right at two of them, leaning over the railing at the far end of the deck. I bopped over there, playing it cool.

"Hello, ladies," I said, in my smoothest imitation of Joe. I lifted my lemonade, making a little toast—and it sloshed out of the glass, splashing all over my white shorts!

I don't know what it is, but I totally lose my cool whenever I get within six feet of a pretty girl. And two of them at once? Forget it.

The girls both put their hands to their mouths to hide their giggles. I tried to think of something funny to say, something that would erase the lame first impression I'd just made.

Before I could think of anything, two good-looking young guys came over to them and started flirting. Suddenly, it was like I'd totally disappeared. No one so much as looked at me.

Rats! I'd blown my chance to interrogate the perfect witnesses—and embarrassed myself besides.

Now I had to go back up to the room and change. There was no way I could talk to *anyone* with my shorts looking like this.

I went back through the bar. It was really crowded now. I had to weave through all the people between me and the lobby. I passed through the open door to the side hallway and started up the stairs.

As I reached the second floor, I heard a door on the floor above me softly open and close.

Wait a minute, I thought. That sound had come from right where our room should be. . . .

"Joe?" I called.

No answer. *Hmm . . .*

I climbed the rest of the stairs to our floor. There was no one around. It must have been someone going into a room, not out of one, or surely I would have seen them.

Right?

I took out my key and opened the door. "Joe?" I called again.

Nothing. I went inside.

Everything seemed normal—except that I didn't remember either me or Joe leaving our window wide open. I went over to it and peered outside.

To my right was a drainpipe, covered with an enormous hanging vine. I leaned out and tried to see if anyone was climbing down—but I couldn't get a really good look without actually climbing out onto the drainpipe myself.

I decided against it. If someone had tried to snoop on us (the bartender, maybe? I hadn't seen him on my way back through the bar)—I'd interrupted their search before it even began.

I changed shorts, rinsed out the yellow stain as best I could, and was about to go back downstairs when I heard a soft knocking at the door.

"Who is it?"

"It's me, Jenna. Remember me, from the smoothie stand?"

"Oh! Sure!" I almost ran to the door to open it, I was so happy to hear her voice.

"Hi, there," she said, giving me a smile that made my knees go rubbery.

"Hi." I gave her a stupid little wave of my hand. "What's up?"

That was all I could think of to say? "What's up?"

Luckily, Jenna didn't seem to notice. "Are you busy?" she asked.

"Me? No, not at all!"

"Can I . . . come in?"

I realized that I was standing in the doorway, blocking her way. I moved aside for her. "Sure! Come on in. I was just heading downstairs, actually."

"Oh. Well, don't let me stop you if you have someplace to go."

"No, no. I was . . . I was just going to go see if I could find *you*. I . . . looked for you a few minutes ago, but you weren't around."

"I just now got off work," she explained. "I do the books at the end of the day, so I was back in the office."

She went over to the window and looked out at the harbor and the twinkling lights of St. Thomas in the distance. "Nice night."

"Definitely. It . . . it really is paradise here."

"Well, yes and no," she said mysteriously.

"Huh? What do you mean?"

"Oh, nothing. It's just that when you live here, it's different somehow. It's still a great place to be, but, well . . . it's a small island. When something exciting happens, everybody's all over it. Know what I mean?"

I had no clue what she was talking about. I would have asked her what she meant, but I didn't want to look like an idiot.

"Would you like to sit down?" I asked.

"Thanks." She settled on the side of the bed nearest the window.

"So . . . how long have you been here?" I said, with my typical lack of cool.

"Two years. During my freshman year of college, I came down to work over the winter break, and just . . . never left. I mean, it's paradise, y'know?"

"Oh, yeah," I agreed, staring into her eyes. "Paradise. Definitely."

"And you? Is this your first time?"

"Huh?"

"On St. John."

"Oh! Uh, yeah. Never been here before."

"And you're with your brother. . . ."

"Yeah. Joe. He's a year younger than me."

"Where is he, anyway?"

I laughed. "Oh, he's downtown, checking out the scene."

I let her think Joe was just looking to meet girls. I didn't tell her what he was *really* looking for—evidence in the hunt for Esteban Calderon.

"I see," she said, her lips curling into a sly smile. "And . . . you didn't go with him?"

"I'm . . . shyer than Joe."

"Aw . . . I think that's so sweet." She leaned in and kissed me on the cheek. "*You're* sweet."

I was paralyzed. I just absolutely could not move.

"Are you okay?" she asked.

"Uhh . . ." I swallowed hard. "Yeah. I'm fine. It's just . . . the heat. I'm not used to it."

"You want to go up to the roof? Get some air?"

"Sure!" I leaped to my feet and escorted her out into the hallway and up the stairs.

There was a tiny garden up on the roof—and in one corner, a bubbling hot tub just big enough for two.

"So, you and your brother came down just for vacation?" Jenna asked.

"Uh-huh," I lied—convincingly, I hoped.

She looked right through me again. I wondered how I could bring up the subject of Esteban

Calderon without giving away my mission.

"So," I began, "a lot of interesting people must come through here, huh?"

"Oh, yeah," she said. "We get movie stars sometimes. And a couple of NFL players stayed at the hotel last winter."

"Diplomats, too?" I asked.

She tilted her head to one side. "Oh. You must have heard about that guy going missing. Ugh."

"Ugh?"

She rolled her eyes. "The police and FBI were all over this place for days. I was so glad when it finally quieted down."

"Did they ever find him?"

"No. Not yet."

She leaned over the railing, staring out at the harbor lights. "He probably drowned or something. It happens every few years—someone goes swimming or diving and doesn't come back. The currents around here are pretty strong—and there are lots of sharks, of course."

I leaned over next to her, and we stood there, side by side. On the one hand, I was really attracted to this girl—and I got the feeling she felt the same way.

On the other hand, I had to find out what she

knew about the case, even if it made me seem unromantic.

"So, how long was he here at the hotel before he went missing?" I asked, staring out at the night.

Luckily, she didn't seem to notice my discomfort. "Oh, a long time. I think he was here for about ten days before it happened—he had an open-ended reservation."

"Mmmm," I said, hoping she'd keep talking.

"Esteban—well, let's just say he made a big impression," Jenna said, smiling. "He was a real party animal. A couple of times he came back to his room at six in the morning, singing at the top of his lungs." She laughed. "I happened to be on late duty those nights. Believe me, it wasn't easy to quiet him down."

"What was he singing?"

She giggled again. "I don't know, it was in Spanish."

Then she stopped laughing. She turned to me and looked right through me. "What do you care, anyway? He's not here, and we are."

She reached up and pushed my hair back off my forehead. I knew if I was going to kiss her, this was the moment. The thought of it was almost enough to distract me from my purpose—but not quite.

"I'm curious," I said. "Did anything unusual happen during his stay?"

"Are you still on that?" she asked, backing off. I could tell she was a little annoyed.

"Sorry," I said. "But if anyone noticed something unusual, it would probably be someone like you."

She crossed her arms in front of her. "What are you, a cop or something?"

I could tell she was joking, but she was getting too close to the truth for comfort. "No, but I'm into detective books and stuff. Just play along with me for a minute, okay?"

She shrugged, but she gave me a little smile. "Go on, then."

"If I *was* a cop, and I told you that any little thing you noticed might save a man's life, what would you say?"

She thought for a moment. "I'd say . . . the most unusual thing was that he had visitors the night before he disappeared."

Yes! Pay dirt!

"Visitors?" I repeated, trying to sound casual. "What kind of visitors?"

"Well, I'd never seen them before, but the reason I noticed is because . . . well, I would have crossed the street to avoid them, you know what I mean?"

"Mmm . . . wow." I wanted her to keep on talking—every detail counted.

"One had a scar on his face that was really hideous—like he'd been cut with a dull knife. And the other was just really ugly—and I don't usually say that about people, but he was so mean-looking—with dead eyes."

"Mmmm."

"The thing that really made me notice was that they weren't the kind of guys you'd expect to see with Esteban. He always dressed well. Seemed like he had money and some class. Not like those two guys he brought up to the room with him that last night—and at one a.m., no less."

"Hmmm . . ."

"So, is that what you meant by 'unusual'?"

"Yeah," I said. "Yeah, that's the kind of thing I had in mind. Anything else?"

"Nothing I didn't tell the police and the FBI." She closed her eyes for a moment and sighed. "Like I said, I'm glad all that's over with—it's no fun being grilled."

I got her meaning loud and clear—she wanted me to change the subject, *now*.

"So you didn't tell the police about the two mean-looking guys?"

She shook her head slowly, and I saw that her lip was trembling.

"Why not?" I asked.

She looked around, just to make sure no one else had come up onto the roof. "Can I trust you?" she whispered.

"Sure!"

"You won't tell anybody? Not even your brother?"

"Mmm," I said, not wanting to make a promise I couldn't keep. Whatever she told me, I would definitely have to share with Joe.

Anyway, she seemed to take my "mmm" for a yes.

"I got a phone call . . . the next night . . . after the police found Esteban's abandoned jeep," she said.

"A phone call?"

"I was working in the office. The police had just come by the hotel and were going through his room, looking for clues. The phone rang, and it was this—this horrible, whispery voice, saying, 'Keep your mouth shut, if you want to live.' "

"Do you think it was one of those two mean-looking guys you saw?"

She shrugged. "I don't know. I never heard them say anything." A little sob forced its way out of her throat. "I—I can't believe I'm telling you all this. I don't know why, but I think I can trust you. I—I had to tell someone. It's been eating me alive."

"I understand, totally. Your secret is safe with me."

"Do you think I should have told the police?"

"It's all right," I said. "You'll be all right."

"I've been so afraid. . . ."

"Don't worry—I'll protect you."

She smiled at me and ran her hand over my cheek. "You really are sweet."

Leaning forward, she kissed me lightly on the cheek.

I thought I was going to die right there and then—but I fought off the urge to kiss her back. I'd just uncovered some potentially major clues in this case—and I wasn't going to just leave them hanging.

"What room was he staying in, by the way?" I asked.

She backed away, staring at me, eyes wide. "You *are* a cop!"

"No! No, no. I'm just . . . well, my brother Joe and I, we're sort of amateur detectives," I admitted. "So when we read about this kidnapping or whatever, at the same hotel where we had reservations, naturally we were curious."

She took a moment, deciding whether or not to believe me. "It was room seventeen, on the second floor in the other wing," she said. "But you can't go in there—they sealed it off as a crime scene."

"Oh."

"Frank," she said, taking my hand. "It's our secret, right? What I told you?"

"I promise, Jenna. You have my word."

"Thank you."

"But tell me one last thing. You don't really believe Esteban died accidentally, do you?"

A shadow seemed to creep over her face, and her expression darkened. She shook her head slowly and looked down at the ground.

"Me neither," I said.

We went back downstairs and said good-bye outside the door to my room. "See you tomorrow?" I asked.

She gave me another melting smile. "Mmm-hmm." Leaning over, she kissed me once more on the cheek, then went quickly down the stairs.

I fished my key out of my pocket and opened the door. Right away I realized—*something was different.*

Both Joe's and my bags had been opened and their contents tossed all over the beds and the floor.

Someone had been in here while I was up on the roof!

5.
The Shadows Creep Closer

I wasn't the least bit convinced there was anything to this case. As far as I was concerned, this guy Esteban was just some super-rich party animal who'd gotten happy feet and decided to get away from it all for a while.

I could picture myself in his shoes—paparazzi chasing him everywhere he went, people trying to make friends with him because they wanted something from his rich, famous father. The urge to disappear must have been strong.

Still, you'd think the police, or at least the FBI, would have found some trace of him by now. Since ATAC had been called in, it meant they hadn't.

It also meant that, if Esteban had disappeared on

purpose, he'd done a really professional job of covering his tracks.

So . . . maybe he'd had some professional help? Like, of the criminal kind?

I wandered the streets of Cruz Bay, trying to put myself in Esteban's shoes on that last night he'd been seen. I followed the sounds of reggae and ska music coming out of the doorways of clubs and nightspots.

If I were a rich young guy like Esteban, which one would I have walked into?

I started flashing Esteban's picture to people at the various clubs. It had been nine days now since his disappearance, so a lot of the tourists who had been here with him had gone home by now. So I concentrated on people who looked like locals—you know, slow-moving people with deep, leathery tans.

I finally had some luck at Rasta Pete's. The bartender, a fine-looking blonde named MaryAnn, told me Esteban had been a regular after I described him. "He was a really good tipper," she said. "I think he liked me, y'know?"

"I'm sure he did," I said. "But was he here on the night of the eighteenth?"

That was the night he'd gone missing.

"Uh-huh." MaryAnn leaned over the bar, so that I could hear her over the music, which was really blasting away.

"Was he alone?" I asked.

"Well, yeah—for a while." She made a face, like she was trying hard to remember.

"What do you mean, 'for a while'?"

"These two other guys came in—well, they didn't really come in, it was more like they stood in the doorway. Esteban was right in the middle of flirting around with me, you know? And then he sees these two guys, and it was like, *whoa*. He paid, and left right away."

"With the other two?"

"I'm not sure. Those guys were already gone by the time he paid. But they could have been waiting for him right outside."

"Would you say Esteban's mood changed when he saw the men?"

"I'll say! It was like a dark cloud came over him—he forgot all about flirting with me, just like that!" She snapped her fingers for emphasis.

"Just like that, huh?"

Hmmm. Maybe there was something to this kidnapping theory after all.

"Say, what are you, a detective or something?" she asked me, giggling.

"Me? Nah—just curious."

"Hey, curiosity killed the cat, y'know. Better be careful who you talk to."

Huh? Was she threatening me?

No, no way—she was just kidding around, I could tell by the expression on her face.

Still, her words sent a chill through me. If word got around that Frank and I were looking into the disappearance—and word was bound to spread, on an island as small as this—things could heat up for us in a hurry.

Other customers came up to the bar, and MaryAnn went over to take their drink orders. I found myself a table—centrally located—and tried to home in on the conversations going on all around me.

It seemed like Esteban's disappearance was not the main topic. Instead, everyone was talking about some sunken ship that had recently been discovered in the waters nearby.

I caught some snippets—"*Santa Inez* was her name"; ". . . they say skeletons were still shackled to the deck. . . ."; ". . . worth a bundle . . ."—but it was way too noisy in Rasta Pete's to make much sense out of it.

I had another idea.

Going back outside, I wandered through the

downtown area until I found a grocery store that was open. "Do you sell newspapers?" I asked the old lady sitting on a wooden crate at the entrance.

"Why you don't wait till mornin'?" she suggested. "Get a fresh one. These here from today."

"That's okay—even better, in fact. Here you go." I fished in my pocket and gave her a five-dollar bill.

"I gotta get you change," she said, starting to get up.

"That's okay, keep it," I told her, grabbing three or four back editions of the local paper, *The Island Gazette.*

Then I went over to the park that separated the restaurant area from the port. I found a bench with a streetlight overhead, took a seat, and settled down to do some research.

Surprisingly, I didn't find anything on the front page about the disappearance of Esteban. On the other hand, there were lots of references to the discovery of the wreck.

Here's what I managed to piece together: The *Santa Inez* was a Spanish galleon—a humongous ship for its day and age (the late1500s). She'd been found in a deep-water trench between two coral reefs, about twelve miles north of St. John.

There was a lot of arguing going on among the

Spanish, British, and American governments about which country had the rights to any treasure found on board. In the meantime, the U.S. Coast Guard and the National Park Service had been keeping watch over the site, to make sure bounty hunters didn't move in and steal it all before it could be counted.

The articles hinted that some theft might already have taken place. A box of coins called doubloons, dating back to the exact year of the ship's sinking, had been seized in New York. The police in Miami had recovered a silver wine flask with SANTA INEZ engraved on it and a sword inscribed with the name of the ship's captain.

According to the papers, diving in the area of the wreck was extremely dangerous, because of swift currents and schools of hungry sharks. The articles warned readers to stay away, under threat of arrest by the coast guard or park rangers.

There were a few updates on the back pages about Esteban, too—mostly saying that police and the FBI were following up leads, but that as yet there had been no break in the case.

I knew why the articles had been buried that way—no one on this beautiful island wanted tourists to be scared away. It was the same reason that rumors about a sunken treasure ship were plastered all over the front page—in order to lure more curious tourists down here.

I wondered if Esteban Calderon had read about the *Santa Inez.* Could his trip down here, and his subsequent disappearance, have had anything to do with the ship's discovery?

"Joe!"

I put my paper down. Frank was running toward me, looking worried.

"Hey, bro—what's up?" I asked.

"Someone's been in our room," he said.

"Anything missing?"

"Not that I could see."

"Hmmm. They didn't take our credit cards and cash, huh?"

"Nope. Maybe they don't care about our money."

That bothered me. It meant that my previous theory—that Esteban had taken off for his own reasons—didn't hold up. It meant his disappearance might really be a kidnapping.

It also meant that someone knew we were here to look into it.

Not good news.

I told Frank about the sunken treasure ship.

"You think there's a connection?" he asked.

"I have no idea. I know one thing, though—money makes people do some pretty awful things."

"Like kidnapping?"

"Oh, definitely."

"Even murder?"

"You said it, I didn't." But I'd thought it.

"That would be bad," Frank said.

"It sure would. But hey, look on the bright side—nobody's found any bodies yet. This gig could work out just fine."

"Hmm. What are the odds?"

I thought about it. "I'm not a betting man, mind you—but if I were, I wouldn't play this hand."

Frank sat next to me on the bench, his elbows resting on his knees, his chin in his hands.

"Hey, bro, cheer up," I told him. "It's a crime to be bummed out when you're in paradise."

"I'm not bummed out," he said. "I'm just thinking."

"About what?"

"About that girl, Jenna."

"Frank's got a cru-ush," I sang softly.

"Cut it out, Joe," he said, his face serious and worried. "She told me something . . . something that affects the case."

"Oh, yeah? What?"

"She saw Esteban with two other guys that night. Mean-looking guys. But she didn't tell the police after the disappearance, because she got a threatening phone call warning her not to talk."

"Oooh. Lead number one," I said. Obviously, it had to be the same two guys MaryAnn saw at Rasta Pete's. "Well, that seals it. We're definitely dealing with some kind of major crime here."

"I would not disagree with that," he said. "So now what do we do?"

"Well, I don't know about you, but I still haven't had my dinner. Let's go have some food for thought."

We picked out a place called Vi's Snack Shack. It was tiny, funky, and open to the park. Vi, a middle-aged lady with a permanent smile on her face, was both the owner and our waitress.

"How y'all doin'?" she asked.

"Fine, fine," we said.

"What a beautiful night, huh?"

"Oh. Yeah," we said.

"We got johnnycake, curried goat, and meat pies."

"What kind of meat?" I asked.

"Goat."

"Anything else?" Frank asked.

"Smoothies. Sodas. Lemonade."

"I'll have the johnnycake," I said. "And a lemonade."

"Me too," Frank said.

"The meat is good," she assured us. "Johnnycake ain't enough for two growin' boys!"

"We're not that hungry," Frank explained.

"Um, Vi—do you know anything about that sunken ship?" I asked her. "You know, the one everybody's talking about?"

"I know ain't nobody s'posed to go divin' out there," she said. "Park rangers tellin' everyone to stay away." Then she laughed. "But some people goin' anyhow."

"Yeah?" I asked. "Who in particular?"

"Oh, I ain't sayin'," she said, still laughing. "You boys gonna get me in trouble. Ha!"

She went to get our johnnycakes and lemonade. When she came back with them, she said, "You boys eatin' dessert for dinner. 'Tain't healthy. Sure you don't want some nice curried goat?"

"Not this time," I said.

Just the thought of it totally killed my appetite. It made me think of the live goats I'd seen all over Cruz Bay. People around here kept them as pets, but they doubled as garbage disposal units—and apparently, as dinner, too!

After we'd eaten our dinners—which really *were* desserts—I went up to the counter to pay the check.

"Um, listen, Vi, my brother and I want to go diving out there—you know, check out the wreck. You think you could hook us up with a dive boat?"

"Oh, I don' know," she said. Her smile was still there, but it was looking mighty shaky.

"We can pay," I assured her.

"How much?"

"Plenty." I took out our wad of cash and waved it in the air. Then I peeled off a twenty and handed it to her. "That's an advance on your share. You can find us at the Buccaneer's Lair. Joe and Frank Hardy."

After we'd left the restaurant, Frank asked me what in the world I thought I was doing.

"If you want to draw flies, you've got to spread around some honey," I told him. "We need to see if there's a connection between the sunken treasure and our missing person."

"And?"

"And, any boat captain who takes people diving out there is risking arrest. People who are willing to do that—well, they tend to know about all kinds of things. If there's a criminal underworld on this island, they might be connected to it."

"Joe, did it ever occur to you that this could be dangerous?"

That Frank—he's such a worrier.

"I already thought of that," I said. "We give them an advance payment, but we don't pay them the rest of the money until we're safely back in Cruz Bay."

"And where do we stash all our valuables, since our room doesn't seem to be safe?"

"I thought of that one, too. We bury them under a tree."

"You really are out of your mind, Joe."

"Hey, watch it. You're not the only brother with ideas, you know. Trust me on this one—if it doesn't go well, next time we'll do it your way."

"If there *is* a next time."

We went back to our room, retrieved our cash, credit cards, wallets, and everything else of value that we'd brought along. Then we walked down the road to the edge of town.

"See that tree over there?" I pointed to a royal palm at the edge of the road. In the moonlight, it almost seemed to glow. "Time to bury a little of our own treasure."

"You think we'll be able to find it later?"

"Dude," I said "Don't insult my sense of direction."

We buried the big zipper-lock plastic bag containing our valuables and headed back to the hotel. We were just climbing the stairs to our room, when a rumbling voice called out to us from the bottom landing.

"Ahoy, there!"

We turned around to look at the face attached to that booming sound. He was about thirty and so tanned that his skin was like leather, and his blond hair, bleached by the sun, was tied back in a long, scraggly ponytail. His barrel of a body was stuffed into a Hawaiian shirt and a huge pair of shorts, and he wore a pair of old rope sandals on his feet.

"Heard you were lookin' for a captain to take you out for a sail," he said. "Name's Corbin. Corbin St. Clare. But you can call me Cap'n." He tipped his grimy sailor cap in salute.

I wondered whether he'd followed us, and whether he'd seen where we'd buried our cash, credit cards, and IDs.

"I can take you out first thing in the morning," he went on. "For the right price, of course."

"What about diving equipment?" Frank asked.

"All included," said Cap'n, giving us a gap-toothed grin. "I'll meet you down at the far dock, five a.m. Fair enough?"

SUSPECT PROFILE

Name: Corbin St. Clare (alias "Cap'n")

Hometown: Unknown

Physical description: Age 30, 6' 2", 260 lbs.; leathery suntanned skin; piercing, squinty blue eyes; long, scraggly blond hair tied in a ponytail; the voice and way of speaking of an old-time pirate.

Occupation: Dive boat captain

Background: A lifelong sailor, he grew up on boats around the port of New Orleans. Raised in a local orphanage, he ran away to sea at age thirteen.

Suspicious behavior: Willing to lead the boys on an illegal dive for the right price.

Suspected of: Being part of the island's criminal underworld.

Motives: That's an easy one-the money.

A young couple appeared—on their way upstairs. They gazed into each other's eyes, barely noticing the three of us.

We waited till they were gone and the stairway was deserted again. "How much?" Frank asked.

"Ah, well," said the captain, "we can sort that out in the mornin'. But it's gonna cost you—these dive trips don't come cheap, y'know."

Especially when they're illegal.

"See yez there," he said, tipping his cap. Then he left, making his way out through the hotel lobby.

"Well," Frank said, "he doesn't exactly inspire confidence, does he?"

"Aw, relax, bro," I said, clapping him on the shoulder. "You've got to stop worrying so much. It's not good for your health."

The next morning Frank's portable alarm clock jarred us awake at four thirty. The sky outside the window was still pitch-black. I slammed my fist down on the alarm until it stopped, then fought off the strong urge to go right back to sleep.

Frank was already up and pulling on his bathing suit. "I've never gone treasure diving before," he said, sounding disgustingly cheerful for that hour of the morning. "Can't wait."

"Wait a minute—just last night, weren't you trying to talk me out of going?"

He just shrugged, and I was too tired to argue

with him. We'd already buried our valuables, so it didn't take us long to get going. We made our way through the deserted town to the dock, getting there just as the first colors of dawn hit the eastern sky.

Cap'n was waiting for us, just as promised. His boat, the *Leaky Sieve*, looked to be perfectly named.

Suddenly, I was the one who felt like bagging the whole idea. But I couldn't back down now—how would that look? Frank would think I was nuts, not to mention a wimp!

"Good to go?" our host asked us.

"Ready," Frank said.

"Me too," I lied. "Let's do this thing."

We shoved off, and the *Leaky Sieve* puttered out into the harbor. We rounded the cape and hung a right, heading out toward the reef that protects St. John's northern shoreline.

Ahead of us, the morning sun broke over the horizon. To our left was a series of small islets that looked uninhabited. To our right was St. John.

"That's Caneel Bay Resort," Cap'n said, pointing to the famous luxury resort, the island's only major hotel. "If you can afford to stay there, you don't need to go diving for sunken treasure."

"Speaking of which," I said, "we never did settle on a price."

"Oh. Right."

He sounded as if he'd forgotten all about it—as if money didn't even matter to him. Weird . . .

"Guess we'd better agree on a price, eh? How does five hundred sound?"

"Five hundred!" Frank shouted. "Are you nuts?"

"Oh, but think of how much you can bring up from the bottom!" Cap'n said, giving us a leering smile. "Just one gold doubloon and you come out ahead, maties!"

Maties? What was this guy, a pirate?

He sure looked the part. If I didn't know it was the twenty-first century, he'd have had me convinced.

"Make it three hundred," I said, all business.

"Four."

"Done."

"Joe!" Frank complained, but I held up a hand to silence him.

"Hey—this is my show, remember?"

"Whatever," he grumbled, shaking his head.

"Up front," Cap'n said.

"No way," I countered. "Fifty now, the rest when we're back in Cruz Bay."

He squinted his eyes at me. "I said up front, or we turn back to port."

"Fifty's all I've got on me," I said. It was true, too.

I pulled the crisp new bill out of my pocket. Then I turned my pockets inside out to show him I wasn't lying. "See?"

Cap'n turned to Frank, and Frank did the same. There was nothing in our pockets, of course—just the way I'd planned it.

"Ah, all right," Cap'n said, sitting back down and taking the wheel again. "It doesn't matter anyway, long as I gets paid."

"That's the spirit," I told him.

We passed beaches so gorgeous they could have been in movies. Then I realized—they *were* in movies. If you've ever seen a film that takes place on a perfect beach, it was probably filmed on St. John.

"That's Trunk Bay," Cap'n yelled over the noise of the motor, pointing to the shore. "There's an underwater snorkeling trail there—but where I'm taking you, it's much more *interesting*."

He winked knowingly.

We turned left, passing over the reef and out between two small islets. We kept going, until there was no land on the horizon in any direction. A little farther out and another reef appeared, a dark patch in the middle of all that beautiful turquoise water.

"Here we are," Cap'n said, tossing the anchor overboard and cutting the motor. "Your gear's back there by the stern—time to suit up."

We put our wet suits on, complete with flippers, air tanks, equalizers, and masks.

"You're good for an hour down there, but don't get trapped inside the wreck—I assume you're certified for wreck diving?"

"Uh, sure!" I said quickly.

We weren't—but we were both fairly experienced divers. I figured we could handle it.

"The current's pretty fierce, so don't let yourselves drift," he warned. "Oh, and if the coast guard or the Park Service come around, I'll have to take off."

"WHAT?" we both shouted at once.

"Just for a little while, maties. Till they leave. Then I'll come back again to get you. I'll be just the other side of that little island we passed before, lying low. They don't hang around for too long—soon as they go, I'll be back."

Frank gave me a look, to see if I was okay with that plan. I wasn't, really, but what choice did we have? If we wanted to get to the bottom of Esteban's disappearance, we had to see if there was a link to the sunken wreck.

"We're good to go," I said. "Frank?"

"Ready."

We dropped off the side of the boat and let ourselves down along the wall of the reef. Suddenly, we were surrounded by bursts of color—a rainbow of coral and sea life so dazzling that for a minute, I forgot all about the wreck.

But there it was, resting on the bottom, just beyond the reef and about thirty feet deeper. It was partly buried in sand, but there were openings in the rotting wooden hull through which we could fit.

I waved to Frank, then led him down and inside the wreck. Using the lights on our masks, we were able to survey the inside of the massive ship.

Everywhere we looked, there were wooden treasure chests. Most of them were smashed open, and many were empty. There were gold coins scattered everywhere along the sandy bottom.

Someone had been here before us, and had made away with a whole lot of plunder!

Then, as my light played further into the darkness, I saw a skeleton—with an iron band around its skinny ankle and another around its neck, chained to what used to be a wall. *Not* a pretty sight.

The thought that went through my head was, was this guy a four-hundred-year-old prisoner of the Spanish galleon and her crew?

Or was it a freshly picked corpse of twenty-first-century vintage?

Esteban Calderon, maybe?

I pointed up to the surface, to tell Frank I thought we'd seen enough. He nodded, and we made for the hole through which we'd entered the wreck.

Just as I was about to leave the skeleton behind, I saw the glint of something silver in the sand at its bony feet. I dove down to retrieve it, then showed it to Frank.

It was a thick chain of real silver—modern, not old at all—with a big, heavy medallion attached. The medallion was engraved with a coat of arms and the initials "E. de V. C."

I didn't know about the "de V." part, but E.C. could easily have stood for Esteban Calderon.

Had he been down here? Maybe he'd drowned on a dive and been swept out to sea by the strength of the current!

Or maybe that skeleton was *him.*

I stuffed the medallion—our first potential piece of evidence—into my pocket.

I would have stayed around to hunt for more, but

our air was starting to run short. I gave Frank a signal, tapping my wrist where my watch would have been. He nodded, pointing upward.

We left the wreck, and rose slowly along the wall of the reef. I broke the surface first, followed seconds later by Frank. I took off my mask and looked around at the open sea.

The open, *empty* sea.

The *Leaky Sieve* was nowhere in sight!

"Uh, Joe?" Frank said.

"He probably had to take off, like he said, because of the coast guard or the park rangers."

"Then where are they?"

Good question.

If there were no coast guard or park service boats around, then why had Cap'n taken off without us?

I remembered how he didn't seem all that interested in the money until we brought it up. It suddenly dawned on me that maybe we'd fallen into a deadly trap. If someone didn't want us nosing around, what better way to get rid of us?

"We're alone out here, Frank," I said.

"Wrong," he said. "We're not alone, Joe. Look over there."

About a hundred yards away, but closing fast,

was a triangular black fin, rising just above the surface.

"SHARK!" Frank screamed.

No, duh. Like I needed him to tell me that.

FRANK

6.
Jaws of Death

Sheesh!

There's nothing like a shark coming at you to focus your mind.

"Stay close together!" I yelled.

I knew that, to a shark, Joe and I would look like a much bigger fish if we stuck together. Sharks don't take on prey that's bigger than they are—not unless they're very, very hungry, that is.

This shark made a quick pass, then started doing slow circles around us. That was good news, I figured—he must have been at least a little nervous about attacking us.

But as the minutes went by, the shark was joined by a bunch of his friends. Soon there were dozens of them—and the circle of fins around us was getting smaller, and tighter, and closer, by the minute.

I kept scanning the horizon, looking for Cap'n and his boat, but they were nowhere in sight. "How long since we surfaced?" I asked Joe.

"About ten minutes?"

"That guy's not coming back for us, is he?"

"Maybe he just can't find us, Frank."

"I don't think so," I said. "We've been set up."

"We could have been drifting all this time. They say the currents are fast around here."

Joe lowered his mask and dove under the surface for a second. "The wreck's nowhere in sight," he said. "He could be looking for us back by the dive site."

I doubted it. But neither of us could doubt that we'd been drifting all this while and had no idea where we were, or where we were headed.

The fins were close now. One shark wouldn't have dared attack the two of us together, but there was now a gang of them—and they would be much braver in a pack.

Our time was running out, and Joe and I knew it. There was no land in sight. Nothing but us, and fins, and . . .

. . . that red thing, sticking up out of the water in

the distance, getting closer by the second.

A buoy!

"Joe!" I shouted, pointing toward it. We swam for all we were worth, the current helping us along—it really was fast here. The buoy seemed to rush at us.

Just as we were about to reach it, I felt something grab my rubber flipper and tug hard.

I shook my leg frantically, and the flipper pulled free. "Jaws" thrashed around, trying to bite the flipper in half.

He was welcome to it, I thought, as I climbed onto the buoy. Joe grabbed onto the opposite side, and we both held on for dear life.

"Now what?" he asked.

"Now we wait until somebody spots us."

"Great. Just great."

"Hey—it's better than being shark food."

The sharks hadn't given up on having us for breakfast—not by a long shot. I took off my remaining flipper and batted them away as best I could, but they were persistent.

Finally, after what seemed like endless hours of shark-swatting, a boat came into view over the horizon. I saw with relief that it was not the *Leaky Sieve*—it was far too big for that.

Good. The last thing we wanted was for Cap'n to come back and finish us off. No, this was a National Park Service boat.

"Boy, are we glad to see you!" Joe greeted the crew.

"What are you boys doing out here?" the captain asked, frowning.

"Our dive boat left without us!" I told him as we climbed aboard and took off our air tanks and masks.

"You must have drifted a ways," the captain said. He looked at the circle of fins. "Those sharks look hungry. Lucky you found that buoy."

"I'll say," Joe agreed.

It turned out that the Park Service boat was on its way back from checking up on the site of the wreck, to make sure no one was stealing the treasure it carried.

On the way back to port, we got to know the captain, whose name was Tom Rollins. We asked about Esteban's disappearance—he didn't know much—and about the wreck of the *Santa Inez*, about which he knew a lot more.

"She went down in a storm in 1583," he said, "loaded with the gold of the Spanish Main and headed for Algeciras. Hurricane took her down the very first day, on a reef just about twelve miles out, just before the international line where U.S. territory ends. She lay there unnoticed for more than four hundred years."

"And since the discovery?" I asked.

"Stuff seems to have gone missing," he said, "but it's hard to know how much has been taken. That's why I've been doing these patrols, five times a day and twice overnight. Just in case."

"Man, that must be pretty time-consuming," I said. "How do you get all your regular jobs done?"

He gave a cheerless laugh. "I don't. We're so understaffed it's a joke. Federal money tends not to make it this far from Washington. I've had to cancel the daily Reef Bay Trail hikes because the boat's too busy to pick up folks at the bottom of the trail and take them back to town."

I was disappointed to hear it, since I'd marked it down in my guidebook as something I wanted to do on St. John. "Can people hike down anyway, on their own?" I asked.

"No, sorry. We've put a chain across the trail. Too dangerous if anyone got hurt on their way down—it's pretty steep in parts, and we wouldn't know you were down there to come pick you up. No, it's closed until further notice. Been that way for two weeks now, ever since we found those artifacts from the *Santa Inez* up in New York City."

After we'd docked at the far end of the harbor by the National Park Service headquarters, Captain Rollins said, "What was the name of that dive boat you boys went out in?"

"The *Leaky Sieve*," we told him.

"Hmmm . . . not one of the regular dive boats. Never heard of it, in fact. What was the captain's name?"

"He said to call him Cap'n," Joe said.

"But didn't he say his name at the beginning?" I said. "What was it. . . . ? Oh, yeah—Corbin. Corbin St. Clare."

"Hmm," the captain said, stroking his chin. "Not a familiar name . . . and I know just about everyone on this island. Well, I'll check into it. I'm gonna have to pull his license. That's a serious thing, to leave your divers behind. That kind of carelessness can cost lives—it almost cost you yours!"

We told him where he could find us and gave him our cell phone numbers for good measure.

After we left him, we stopped at our palm tree to dig up our stuff, then headed back to the Buccaneer's Lair.

"Well," I said, "at least we know one thing."

"What's that?"

"We've managed to make somebody really nervous."

"The kidnappers?"

"Maybe. Or bounty hunters."

"Or both."

It was the heat of the day, and we both needed a rest after our watery ordeal. As soon as we reached the hotel, we went straight up to our room. I was happy to see that nothing seemed to have been disturbed this time.

"Hey," Joe said, "we should check our voice mail."

We turned on our cell phones, and sure enough, both of us had messages to call Dad.

"I'll do it," I said, hitting the speed dial. "Hello, Dad? It's me, Frank."

"Frank! Where have you boys been? Are you all right?"

"We're fine. What's up?"

"Have you found anything yet?"

"Not much," I admitted. "We're working on a few leads. . . ."

"Well, you'd better pick up the pace," he said. "Señor Calderon is kicking up quite a stink in Washington, demanding his son's safe return immediately."

"Dad, we're definitely onto something down here, but we're not sure what. See, the thing is, if Esteban was kidnapped, where's the ransom note?"

"Uh, Frank . . ."

There was something funny in Joe's voice. I turned around and saw him draw an envelope out from under his pillow.

"Hold on, Dad," I said. "Something just turned up."

Joe opened the envelope and took out a piece of paper. "Pay dirt," he said.

"Okay, let's hear it," I said.

I gave him my phone, and he spoke into it. "You listening, Dad? Good. The note says 'We have Esteban Calderon. Leave the island by midnight tonight and don't come back—or we will kill him. Leave one million dollars cash in your hotel room. He will be released within twelve hours if you cooperate. If not, he will be food for the sharks.' It's not signed," he added.

I grabbed my phone back. "Dad? What do we do now?" I asked.

"I'll have to get back to you," he said, sounding upset. "Give me a couple of hours. Just stay put till then, Frank—do you hear me? Stay out of harm's way. Whoever left that note obviously knows what you're up to."

He hung up.

At this point, Joe and I were both bone tired. We'd been up since four-thirty in the morning and had exhausted ourselves trying to avoid those sharks. Still, if we had to leave the island that night, no way were we going to waste the rest of our last day here sleeping.

I figured that Esteban's father, with all his connections, would be able to raise the dough. But until we heard back for sure, we had to keep on investigating. After all, if we did get lucky, Señor Calderon would save himself a million dollars.

"We've got till midnight," Joe said. "Or till the last ferry, anyway."

I checked in our night table for the ferry schedule. "Last one's at eight p.m.," I said.

"It's almost three now. I say we go pick up our scooter rentals and head out to where they found the abandoned Jeep."

"Dad said stay put," I reminded him. "Still, if we have our phones with us, he can reach us anytime. You think it's okay to go?"

"Most definitely," Joe agreed. "Do you realize we've been here almost twenty-four hours and we still haven't seen most of the island?"

We got our backpacks together, complete with candy bars from the minifridge (hey, ATAC was paying!). Then we went downstairs to the lobby, where Jenna was at work behind the reception counter.

She seemed surprised to see us. "Oh, hey!" she said, waving. "How's it going?"

"We're still in one piece," Joe cracked, but Jenna didn't get the joke. She stared at him like he was loony.

"We're going to rent scooters," I told her.

"Oh, fantastic!" she said. "You're gonna have a great time."

I leaned over the counter and lowered my voice. "I, um, was wondering if you could give us directions to where Esteban's Jeep was found."

"Oh, sure. How's the investigation going?"

"It's going," I said. "But I can't really talk about it yet."

"Oh. Okay," she said, sounding disappointed. "Well, let me know when you can."

She reached across the counter and grabbed my wrist. "Frank," she said, looking me right in the eyes, "should I be scared?"

"No, no," I assured her. "You'll be fine."

But I wasn't so sure. Whoever had warned her against talking to the police would not be happy if they found out she'd confided in me.

"If you sense anything's not right, just call me at this number." I jotted down my cell number, and she tucked it into the pocket of her shorts.

"Thanks," she said, giving me a smile. "That makes me feel better." She wrote down the directions for me, and we waved good-bye.

"Whoo-ee!" Joe whooped as we left the hotel and headed for the rental place. "That girl likes you, brother. And is she *ever* fine!"

"Get out of here," I said, shoving him lightly. "Just change the subject, will you? We're here on serious business."

"Okay, okay," he said. "But you know I'm right."

We picked up our scooters (which were pretty ordinary—not like the supercharged sport bikes we have back home) and headed through town, driving on the left like they do in England.

We passed the National Park Service headquarters, and the tree where we'd buried our stuff. Then we were in new territory. Here, the jungle overgrew the narrow road that wound along the coastline.

We passed Caneel Bay Plantation. This was the area we'd seen from the boat that morning, and it was just as incredible from land.

"Hey, Frank," Joe shouted over the noise of the

scooters, "wouldn't you think Esteban would be staying here, not at the Buccaneer's Lair? I mean, he had money, right?"

"Never assume," I told him. "Just because his father's well connected doesn't mean he's rich. Maybe his father doesn't give him enough to party on."

"Or maybe he wanted to be near where the parties were happening," Joe said.

We passed Trunk Bay, Cinnamon Bay, Maho Bay—one beach more unbelievable than the next. Normally I would have stopped for a swim, maybe even some snorkeling—but we had work to do, and not much time left to do it.

We reached the turnoff for Leinster Bay, where the ruins of the old sugar mill were. "In the old colonial times, slaves were imported to harvest sugar cane here," I told Joe as we pulled over. "Now all that's left are these ruins."

"How do you know all this stuff?"

"I read, bro. Remember, on the plane? The guidebook? You should read a book sometime. You might learn something."

"Ha, ha. Very funny."

The sugar mill had been built from coral bricks. Now they were half crumbled away, and the remaining walls were covered by vines. It made a ghostly impression, even on this sunny day.

The whole place was deserted—not a car or a human being in sight. And it was here, in the small gravel parking lot, that Esteban's rented Jeep had been found, abandoned.

"You don't think he came out here just to look at the ruins, do you?" I said.

"No way," Joe said. "Those two guys he met the night before probably tied him up, threw him into the back of the Jeep, then drove him out here, where they were met by another car—or maybe a boat that took them off the island."

I stared across Leinster Bay to the string of small uninhabited islets we'd passed through that morning. Could Esteban Calderon be out there? Was that his skeleton we'd seen at the sunken wreck?

I remembered something else I'd read on the plane. "This bay was one place where Sir Francis Drake hid his ships. They lay here in ambush, waiting for treasure ships to pass by."

"It's the perfect spot for it," Joe said.

I thought about the sunken Spanish galleon. If that hurricane hadn't sunk it, maybe the English pirates would have.

I wondered again if Esteban had come to St.

John because of that sunken treasure. Maybe he'd been lured out here, into a trap, by people who'd found another, easier way to cash in—by kidnapping him!

7.
Undercover Agents

This place was giving me the creeps. I could almost feel the tortured ghosts of long-dead slaves flying in and out of the holes in the old sugar mill.

Or maybe the creepy feeling was something else. Maybe it wasn't ghosts. Maybe we were being watched by live human beings. I kept looking over my shoulder, trying to catch them in the act, peeking at us from behind a boulder or a palm tree.

"Frank, let's get out of here. There's nothing to find. And I've got a bad feeling about this place."

"Don't worry," he said.

"Don't worry? Somebody already tried to kill us once today. Isn't that enough?"

"I think we're safe, at least till midnight," he said. "Otherwise, how are they going to get their ransom money?"

He had a point. It made me feel better, but only slightly.

"That medallion we found down at the wreck," Frank said, opening up a bag of potato chips and digging into them. "Do you think it was Esteban's?"

I nodded.

"Me too," he said. "It fits the general picture. If Esteban came down here to get himself some treasure, he probably wasn't the only one. If someone else wanted it all for themselves, they might have gotten rid of any competition that came along."

"Then what about the ransom note?" I pointed out.

"Just another way to make some money?" he suggested.

"Then Esteban . . ."

"That's right. He may already be history."

"Still, I'll bet his dad agrees to pay up," I said. "Wouldn't you, if it were your son?"

"You bet I would. Sheesh."

It was getting late in the day, and Dad still

hadn't called back. I wondered why. Pulling out my cell phone, I flipped it open—and saw that there were no bars.

"We're in a dead zone, Frank!"

He opened his phone, just in case. "Great," he said. "Dad's probably been trying to reach us all this time! Come on, we'd better head back to town, where we can get reception."

We hopped back on our scooters and reversed course, back toward Cruz Bay. Just as we got to the royal palm tree where we'd buried our IDs the night before, our reception came back, and both our phones started chirping at once.

"Messages from Dad," Frank said. We pulled over, and Frank called him back.

I stood there waiting while he listened and nodded his head. "So we pick it up, drop it off in our room . . . uh-huh . . . right. If there's a problem, we'll get back to you. Otherwise, we'll call you from St. Thomas when we get there."

He hung up. "The money will be on the seven o'clock ferry," he told me, "as a regular package with our names on it. We're supposed to pick it up, leave it in our room, and take the last ferry to St. Thomas—the eight o'clock one."

I couldn't believe what I was hearing. "So, what?

We're just going to let the kidnappers get away with it?"

He shrugged. "I guess so. Those were Dad's instructions."

"Well, I don't like it. Those guys tried to kill us, Frank."

"How do you know it was those guys? Cap'n could have been just a rival treasure hunter, not a kidnapper."

"You think so? What are the odds, Frank? Remember, we found Esteban's medallion down at the wreck."

"Okay, okay," he said. "But Dad was very clear—"

"Did he say we had to drop the case?"

"Not exactly, but—"

"Well, then. Just listen to my plan before you say no, okay?"

He made a face. "You've got a plan? You?"

"Do you want to hear it or not?"

"Okay, okay. Shoot. Let's hear it."

"Okay, then. We get on the ferry at eight, just like Dad said. Whoever's watching to see that we leave the island, sees us leave the island—except we don't really leave! Just as the ferry's about to pass the cape at the end of the harbor, we jump off and swim back to shore."

"And . . . nobody on the ferry sees us do this?"

"Not if we set off a little diversion at the other end of the boat," I said. "I can rig something up—a smoke bomb or something."

"And what about our bags?" Frank pointed out.

"Ah," I said, lifting a finger in the air, "I've got that covered too—we bury what we need, right here at the tree. Then we stuff our bags with paper so they look full, and take them onto the ferry with us."

"Okay, I get it so far," Frank said. He looked uncomfortable with the whole idea, but that didn't surprise me—he's used to always being the one with the ideas. "But Joe, what's the point?"

"The point is, we're back on the island, but nobody knows we're here. So the kidnappers think they're safe. They go to pick up the loot, and we're watching them, ready to follow them back to their hideout and rescue Esteban if he's still alive. Then we arrest the bad guys."

"Joe, we're unarmed," Frank said. "What are the odds the bad guys don't have any weapons?"

"Um . . . so we call for backup?"

"Chances are we're in a cellular dead zone."

"Well . . ." The truth was, I had no idea what we would do if the kidnappers pulled weapons on us. "I'll come up with something between now and then."

"There's only two of us against however many of them, Joe."

"No—there are three of us. Don't forget Esteban."

"Assuming he's in any condition to help."

"I told you—I'll figure something out, Frank. I promise."

"Okay," Frank said. He didn't look too happy about it, though. "Only because I hate to see anybody get away with kidnapping and attempted murder. And because I don't have any better ideas."

"That's the spirit!" I said. "Now, come on. We've got a lot to do between now and seven o'clock."

We went back to the hotel and stuffed our bags with towels, newspapers, bottles of shampoo—anything to make them seem full. Then we put our valuables in ziplock bags, got back on our scooters, rode out to the tree, and buried them. It was tough with cars passing by every minute, but Frank screened me so I couldn't be seen from the road.

When it was done, we went down to the ferry dock to meet the boat and pick up our "package." As the crowd began to gather, we saw representatives from half a dozen small hotels, carrying signs that welcomed tonight's crop of new visitors.

"Hey," Frank said. "Over there. It's Captain Rollins from the National Park Service—the one who rescued us this morning."

We went over to say hello and to find out if he'd had any luck tracking down Corbin St. Clare, alias "Cap'n."

"Glad to see you boys have recovered," he said.

"Thanks again for your help," Frank told him.

"Aw, just doin' my job."

"Did you run down that lead for us?" I asked.

"I did, but I didn't come up with anything. There's no Corbin St. Clare registered here, or in St. Thomas for that matter. No *Leaky Sieve*, either. You boys must have gone out on a ghost ship."

Neither Frank nor I thought his joke was very funny, but he laughed anyway. "Next time, check the bulletin board over there for the regular charter boats. They're all very reputable."

Yes, I thought, *but a reputable captain wouldn't have taken us out to dive at a wreck that was declared "off-limits."*

The ferry pulled in right on schedule, and we picked up our package—a plain brown box that weighed a ton, considering its size. Let me tell you: Money is heavy when you put enough of it together!

We took the box back to our room and opened it. Inside was a metal briefcase, which I took out and put on the night table. "Should we open it?" I asked.

"I don't think so."

"Why not?"

"Maybe it's booby-trapped or something. If Dad has something up his sleeve, we don't want to mess it up."

"Dad wouldn't pull something like that—not when somebody's life depends on it."

"You're probably right, Joe, but I still think we shouldn't mess with it."

"Okay, okay. Let's do our thing."

It was seven thirty. Time to put our plan into action. I grabbed a pack of matches—very important—stuffed them into my pocket, and we hoisted our backpacks onto our backs. "Let's go," I said.

We tiptoed down the stairs. At the bottom landing, Frank guarded the entrance from the lobby to make sure nobody was looking.

Meanwhile, I went over to the emergency exit and disconnected the alarm, using the miniature screwdriver on my Swiss Army knife. I propped the door open—barely—with a washcloth I'd brought from our room.

Okay, step one was complete. Time to get noisy

and attract some attention, so whoever was watching us would see that we were leaving the island.

We walked into the lobby. That girl Jenna was behind the desk—and you should have seen the look on her face when she saw us.

"You guys are leaving?" she asked, looking really upset. "I thought you were here for a whole week."

"Change of plans," I said. "We're catching the late boat out."

"What happened?" she asked, suddenly nervous. "Is everything okay?"

Frank was squirming, looking from me to her and back to me again. I could tell I was going to have to do the explaining.

"Family problem back home," I lied. "We just got the call this afternoon."

"Oh. So I guess . . . this is good-bye, then."

"I—I guess so," Frank said.

She came around to the front of the counter and gave him a big hug and a kiss on the cheek.

Me, she just turned to and said, "Bye."

Great.

"*Ciao*," I said.

She leaned into Frank's ear, and I heard her whisper, "But what about . . . you know . . . the phone call I got?"

"I don't think they'll bother you anymore," Frank

told her. "I'm pretty sure of it, in fact. After tonight, everything should be settled once and for all."

"Oh. Good . . . I think," she said. "It *is* good . . . isn't it?"

"I think so," he told her. "I hope so."

She still had sort of a scared look in her eyes as we left, heading out through the bar.

This part was Frank's idea—he wanted the bartender to get a good look at us leaving. For some reason, he thought the bartender was in on the plot. He didn't say why he suspected him—just that he thought someone at the hotel had fingered Esteban for kidnapping, and he had a feeling about the bartender.

Still, Frank's crime radar is usually pretty good, so I was more than willing to go along with his exit route.

I have to say, the guy *looked* like a real thug—maybe he was the one who'd fingered Esteban Calderon for kidnapping. I kept an eye on him as we passed through the bar, out the back door, onto the deck, then down the stairs to the street.

He gave us the eye, all right. Which was good—the more people who knew we were leaving, the better.

We got down to the dock with ten minutes to spare, paid for our tickets, and boarded the ferry.

We dropped our backpacks at the front of the boat, where we were hidden from anyone in the passenger area.

"Okay, we're all set," I said, feeling in my pocket to make sure I still had the matches.

There they were. Good.

Promptly at eight, the ferry blew its horn, the crew cast off the ropes, and the boat pulled away.

I scanned the crowd on the dock. Somebody would be watching to make sure we left the island. But in the glare of the setting sun, I couldn't make out any familiar faces.

As soon as we were far enough away, I said, "Watch my back," then went into action.

With Frank blocking the view of any curious passengers, I ran to the front of the boat. Making sure I was hidden from all prying eyes, I whipped out my pack of matches.

I opened my backpack, pulled out the end of a piece of newspaper, and struck a match. Carefully cupping it to protect it from the wind, I lit the piece of newspaper, then tossed the lit match into the backpack. I blew into it softly, helping the paper inside to ignite.

It took a while. For a minute or so, I thought it wasn't going to catch fire in time. We needed to jump off the boat while we were still within swimming distance from the tip of the island, or we might be swept out to sea by the fierce currents in the strait.

Just in time, the backpack caught fire. Smoke billowed upward, and the wind blew it back at the crowd huddled in the boat's midsection. I ran back that way, yelling, "Fire! Fire!"

Everyone erupted in panic. The crew started running forward. Everyone's eyes were on them.

I turned to Frank. "Now's our chance, brother." We ran for the back of the boat, unnoticed.

The cape at the tip of St. John was just on our right—our timing had been perfect. "Three . . . two . . . one . . . jump!" I shouted.

We leaped off the boat and into the surf, then swam across the ferry's wake toward land. We were only about fifty yards from the cape, but the current was pulling us out into the open strait. It was all we could do to fight it.

By the time we reached the rocks and hauled ourselves up out of the water, the ferry had moved into the current. We could still see the smoke, though. The crew was spraying our backpacks with fire extinguishers. They seemed to have things under control, just as I'd expected.

Frank and I were exhausted, but we could only take a moment to catch our breath. Time was running out—we had to get back to the Buccaneer's Lair before the kidnappers came and picked up their money.

We had left dry clothes and shoes by the palm tree, above ground for easy grabbing—and lucky for us, they were still there. We changed into them, then ran back to town as fast as we could.

We got to the Buccaneer's Lair and entered unseen through the emergency door I'd propped open. "Anybody coming?" I asked Frank.

"No. The coast is clear."

We were just about to climb the stairs to our room when we heard a door open and close upstairs.

"Quick! Hide!" Frank whispered.

We both squatted under the stairs by the emergency exit. We waited as the heavy footsteps came down the stairs toward us. They passed right over our heads, then reached the bottom landing.

Peeking out, I saw the back of a green Hawaiian shirt. It was the bartender—and he was carrying the metal briefcase!

FRANK

8.
The Chase Is On

The bartender turned suddenly in our direction. We huddled in the shadow of the stairs and held our breath, hoping he wouldn't look down and see us.

He didn't—he walked right past us, straight to the emergency door. He put down the briefcase and fished out a set of keys to unlock the door. Then he saw that it was already jimmied.

"Huh?" He looked like he didn't know what to think about it—should he go out through the door, or turn back?

Part of me actually hoped he did turn around and see us. I wanted so badly just to jump him—now, when we had a two-to-one advantage. Surely we could take him down, then force him to tell us where they were hiding Esteban.

But I knew Joe's original plan was better. The bartender would lead us straight to his partners in crime, if we just left him alone and followed him.

He grabbed the briefcase, opened the door, then closed it behind him. Joe and I were alone again.

We waited about ten seconds, then slowly cracked open the emergency door. There was our man, just down the street. He seemed to be standing there, waiting for something. Luckily, he was staring away from us, looking down the road toward town.

A pair of headlights pierced the evening darkness. A black Jeep roared up next to the bartender and screeched to a halt. He opened the back door and tossed the briefcase inside.

"Straight to the mill," I heard him say as he got into the backseat, slamming the door shut behind him.

At least, that's what I *thought* I heard.

With a screech of wheels, the Jeep started up again and roared past us. In the front seat were two of the meanest-looking, ugliest guys I'd ever laid eyes on. I knew right away that they had to be the ones Jenna had seen with Esteban the night before he went missing.

"Come on!" Joe said, shoving the door all the way open. "Let's get our scooters and go after them!"

Of course, we both knew that our lame, pathetic scooters stood exactly zero chance of keeping up with the Jeep.

But I thought I knew where they were going. If we just kept after them, we might get to the old sugar mill ruins just a few minutes after they did. Then, if they weren't still there, we could make up time following them on foot.

What other choice did we have, anyway?

We got to our scooters and revved them up. I could still see the Jeep's taillights several blocks away, pulling past the National Park Service headquarters in the direction of the north coast road.

It was the way to Leinster Bay and the old sugar mill.

Lucky for us, the roads on St. John, especially this one, are incredibly winding and narrow. It's tough to go very fast on them, especially in the dark, and even in a Jeep.

We soon lost their taillights, but there were only so many turnoffs from the main coast road. If they tried to go up one of the many steep dirt tracks that led up to houses hidden in the mountains, we'd see the dust cloud they left behind.

There were no dust clouds, so I had confidence we were still on their trail. The only paved turnoffs were the ones leading to Caneel Bay Resort, the luxury hotel (and I was sure they wouldn't be going there), and one leading up to the Centerline Road.

"Which way?" Joe asked when we came to that fork in the road.

"Left," I said. "To the old sugar mill."

It was all I had to go on. If I was wrong, we could always go the other way later. Of course, by then they'd be long gone, but I had to choose—fast.

It was dark, and the roads were really treacherous, winding and twisting, with steep mountainside on the right and palm trees fringing the beaches on our left.

Finally, we reached the ruins of the old sugar mill. My heart sank—the parking lot was empty!

"We've lost them!" Joe said, hitting his handlebars in frustration.

"That guy said 'straight to the mill.' As in, 'take me there right away.'"

"Well, maybe they came, let him out, and left again," Joe suggested.

"I don't think so," I said. "We can't have been more than five minutes behind them."

"Five minutes is enough."

I thought about it. "If they dropped him off, they must have kept going east, toward Coral Bay. Otherwise, we'd have passed them on their way back."

"So? Maybe that's where they went."

"But if they dropped him off, where could he go from here?"

We stared down toward Leinster Bay, the old pirate stomping grounds. There were a few twinkling lights out in the bay—small boats, and a few larger yachts, anchored for the night.

Could our bartender friend have walked down to the beach and been picked up by a boat? The *Leaky Sieve*, maybe? If he had, there was no way for us to follow him.

"Hey, you know what?" Joe said suddenly.

"What?"

"Maybe there's another mill somewhere."

I was stunned. "You know, little brother—you might just have something there!"

What was it I'd read on the plane, in that National Park Service pamphlet? Something about an old sugar mill at the bottom of a trail? I'd circled the page, I remembered that—but the name of the trail escaped me.

One thing was for sure, though—if the Jeep had been going to the other sugar mill, it would have turned right at the fork in the road, heading for the Centerline Road.

That was where the trail started, at the top of the mountain. It was the only way to get to the sugar mill ruins, except by water. Even if they'd gone that way, we had no choice but to approach by land.

"Back to the fork in the road!" I said. Joe and I sprang into action, doing wheelies on our scooters and heading back the way we'd come. We made a sharp left at the fork, then headed up into the mountains.

It was very dark, and we'd never traveled this road before. Our scooters couldn't get up the steep parts very fast. And the road was really narrow, too—hemmed in by rocky mountainside on one side, and sheer cliffs on the other.

We hadn't gone more than a mile when we realized there was a car approaching from behind us. It was gaining on us quickly, and we must have been clear in their headlights.

Soon they'd have to slow down, I thought. Because there was no room on the left for us to get out of the way. And on the right, only a sheer drop through the jungle, who knew how far? We couldn't see a thing down there.

The car slowed down as it got within about fifty feet. I was relieved. At least they saw us. Now they'd just have to be patient, until we reached a spot where we could pull over and let them pass.

All of a sudden there was a screech of tires as the car quickly sped up.

"They're coming right for us!" Joe yelled.

As if I couldn't see that.

We were going as fast as we could, but the car was gaining on us in a hurry.

"Noooo!" we both screamed.

The car was right on us now. I looked back for one brief instant—just to see the face of the person who was about to kill us.

It was none other than Cap'n—good old Corbin St. Clare!

And sitting next to him, looking as terrified as a ghost, was Jenna!

Was she being kidnapped too? They'd already threatened her life once. They must have found out she'd talked to me!

Or was she on their side?

I looked back to the road, and just in time, leaned into another hairpin turn.

We gained a foot or two on the car, but only for a moment. Then the car's front bumper hit our rear wheels, crushing our scooters into scrap metal.

Joe and I were tossed into the air. We tumbled head over heels, landed hard at the edge of the road, then went right over the edge of the cliff.

9.

The Pirates' Lair

Everything hurt. I mean *everything*. I opened my eyes and I couldn't see a thing. For a second I thought I was dead, or at least blind, but then I realized there was a palm leaf covering my face.

I pulled it off me (ah, my arms still worked) and there was the full moon, and the stars, and the tops of the trees.

I was lying on the ground, and my feet were propped against a tree trunk.

"Frank?" I called out.

"Oohhhh . . ."

He was alive, at least. The sound came from my right. I turned my head painfully in that direction, and there he was, caught between the twin trunks of a huge tree. His feet were higher than his head.

"You okay?"

"No. You?"

"No."

"Can you get up?"

"I . . . think so," I said.

Then I tried. It was slow going, since I had to test every body part first to be sure it wasn't broken. I could feel all the black and blue marks on my legs and arms, and I could only imagine what my face looked like. There was a huge bump on my forehead, for sure, from the rock or tree or whatever it was that got me in the face.

"I'm up," I said finally, as I steadied my feet on the steep ground.

"Well, then, come and help me!"

"I'm on my way, bro."

I had to find hand- and footholds, or I'd have slid right down into the darkness. Painfully, slowly, I got to Frank and was able to turn him right side up.

"You okay?" I asked him.

"Ow," he said. "Do I look okay?"

His face was black with dirt, and he had a cut on his ear that was probably going to need stitches. "You've looked better," I said.

"Well, I feel like crud."

"Me too, but we'd better get back up there if we want to catch those dirtbags."

We helped each other climb back up to the road. Pieces of our scooters were strewn everywhere. But at least our attackers were nowhere in sight.

"Maybe we could hitch a ride," Frank suggested.

I looked back at the dark road, lit only by moonlight filtering through the trees. "Not much traffic. We'd better start walking."

Walking was slow, especially since we were going mostly uphill. But it was good for our sore muscles. After a while, I hardly noticed the pain in my arms, legs, and head.

It took us about fifteen minutes to walk to the junction of our road and the Central Highway. We didn't see one single car the whole time. Traffic on St. John's lesser roads was pretty scarce after dark.

There was a sign at the junction: REEF BAY TRAILHEAD, ½ MILE.

"Reef Bay! That's it!" Frank said excitedly.

"That's what?"

"That's where the other sugar mill ruins are—at the bottom of that trail!"

We started jogging, picking up the pace. We both knew there was no time to lose.

"Do you think they'll let Esteban go free now

that they've got the money?" I asked.

"If they were going to let him go, then why take Jenna?"

"I see your point. So you think they'll get rid of them both, to cover their tracks?"

Frank was silent for a moment as he thought about that grim possibility. "Not if we get there in time to stop them."

Ah, but time was ticking by, and it was a good thing a truck came by and gave us a ride to the trailhead.

The driver, a young local guy who did landscaping for the wealthy owners of island vacation homes, asked us if we were sure we wanted to be dropped off at the trailhead, seeing that it was after dark. (We couldn't share with him our reasons for wanting to be there.) "That trail's been closed for two weeks now," he said.

"Making the sugar mill ruins a perfect hideout," Frank whispered in my ear.

I pointed to a pair of cars parked in the small roadside parking area. "That's our lift home," I told our driver.

"Tha's cool, mon. Nice seein' y'all." He took off, and his truck disappeared down the road.

One of the parked cars, a gray sedan, had a badly dented front bumper. "That's the one that ran us down," I said.

The other was the black Jeep we'd followed out of Cruz Bay.

"They're here, all right!" Frank said excitedly. "Let's go after them!"

"Do you think we should call for backup before we start down the trail?" I asked.

We whipped out our cell phones, but of course, we were in another dead zone. "Too late," I said.

So, no backup. We were totally on our own, facing a gang of kidnappers who had already tried to kill us twice. They'd failed both times, but I wasn't sure I liked our chances of surviving a third attempt.

"Joe," Frank said, "that car that tried to run us down—do you think they knew it was us?"

"I guess so," I said. "Or do you think they were just in a hurry and didn't care who they ran down?"

"No. But maybe they didn't know we were still here until that moment when they saw us in their headlights. I mean, it's true, they had Jenna—but she thought we were leaving the island, so they couldn't have found out from her."

"Either way, they know now that we're here," I said, "and that's bad."

"Correction," he said. "They think we died going over that cliff. And that's good."

He was right. They hadn't even stopped to check whether they'd killed us, so they must have felt pretty sure they had.

"Enough time wasted," I said. "Let's get going."

We headed down the trail and into the thick, dark jungle. I heard animals scuttling around the ground, hunting for prey, or trying to escape predators.

We were hunters too—but we had no weapons. If we did succeed in catching up with our band of kidnappers, how exactly were we going to foil their escape?

When Frank had asked me about it, I'd told him I'd come up with something.

What was I thinking? I didn't have a clue. I could only hope for some last-minute inspiration to strike. Remembering my pocket flashlight, I pulled it out and flicked it on.

A few of the trees we passed had identifying markers tacked up on them by the National Park Service. One in particular caught my eye: the strangler fig.

According to the sign, the tree actually starts life as a vine that creeps up the trunk of some other poor tree. The strangler sends down roots from the air, and they wind around the trunk of the original tree. Sooner or later, the strangled tree dies, and the parasite strangler fig is all that's left.

It reminded me of how criminals work—greedily squeezing the life out of innocent people who are just minding their own business. It made me angry, and if I wasn't hurting so badly, I would have given that strangler fig a good kick in the trunk.

Another tree that caught my eye was the monkey-no-climb tree, also known as a monkey puzzle tree—and I could see why. The entire trunk was dotted with sharp little bumps, like spikes. If I was a monkey, I would have picked some other tree to climb for sure.

After about half an hour, I was really getting tired. It had been an exhausting couple of days, and I was beginning to think we'd never catch up to those thugs in time to stop them from killing their captives and getting away.

I needed to stop and rest for a few minutes, but of course, there was no time for resting—not with two innocent lives at stake.

Just as I felt like I was going to collapse, I heard the sound of rushing water up ahead. A moment later, we came to a beautiful waterfall. It gushed out of a rock and went tumbling into a perfect swimming hole.

"Awesome!" I said, emptying my pockets before

jumping in. The cold water was the perfect tonic for everything that was ailing me.

Frank plunged in too—and at least for a minute, we experienced what a paradise this island could really be, when you weren't in a life-and-death struggle with bad guys.

A minute was all we could spare, though. Too bad. I would have loved to spend the whole night there at that waterfall—the whole week, in fact.

"We've got to come back here!" I said.

"Hey, look!" Frank said, pointing to something on the side of the rock where the waterfall emerged. "Petroglyphs," he said. "Ancient rock paintings."

"Whoa. You think they're from the Stone Age?"

"Probably pre-Columbian Indians," he said.

Who was I to argue? Frank's the one who remembers every last thing in every single textbook he ever read.

We took off again, following the trail as it wound downhill toward the beach and the old sugar mill ruins.

About ten minutes later, we started to hear sounds ahead in the distance—human voices! If we had any lingering doubts about whether we were on the right track, they disappeared in that instant.

"Come on!" Frank said, quickening his steps. "They're still here!"

I kept pace, although I still wondered what we were going to do once we got there.

I noticed an orange glow in the sky above the trees up ahead. A bonfire, I guessed. We could tell by the light just how close we were getting. We stopped running when we thought we were in earshot.

The voices were more distinct now—men's voices, all of them. I knew Frank would be listening for Jenna's voice, hoping she was still alive.

I had my doubts. The look on her face in that car had been one of sheer terror.

We crept closer, hiding behind a fringe of bushes. The light from the bonfire made everything look orange and black. In fact, what we saw as we peeked through those bushes was very like Halloween.

The ruins of this old sugar mill were in much worse shape than the ones at Leinster Bay. These had liana vines all over them, and they were crumbling into the sand. They rose up as high as the palms, looking eerie in the orange light.

You could almost imagine ghosts flying out of those empty black holes that had once been windows and doors—just like at the other sugar mill.

Our gang of kidnappers wasn't wearing pirate costumes or anything like that—but they were pirates in every other way. They carried knives in their belts, pistols in their holsters, and machetes in their hands.

And stacked everywhere, all around the ruins, and glowing more brightly than anything else, were piles and piles of gold doubloons and other pirate treasure!

FRANK

10.

Surprise, Surprise

I felt a triumphant surge of energy go through me. We had survived almost certain death, and now we had found the kidnappers' secret hideout.

Somewhere at this remote campsite were Jenna and Esteban—hopefully, both still alive.

I tried to make out people's faces in the orange glow. There was a group of about six men clustered around the flames. They were busy eating chicken legs, ripping them apart and throwing the bones into the fire. The grease threw sparks into the air, but no one seemed too worried about the danger of being burned, much less discovered.

These men knew their fire would not give them away. This side of St. John was completely uninhabited. Their secret campsite was hidden from the world by the mountain on one side, and by the open ocean on the other.

I recognized two of the six men as the mean-looking ones Jenna had talked about. Her description was pretty good, I have to say. The other four I didn't recognize. The bartender from the Buccaneer's Lair was nowhere in sight. Neither was Cap'n, or Jenna, or Esteban Calderon.

I wondered how long they'd been here, collecting their treasure from the wreck of the *Santa Inez*.

I figured that the gang must have set up camp here, knowing that no hikers would be coming their way. No one would disturb their privacy or spy the treasure they were steadily heaping up on the beach.

I thought about the name of our hotel—how perfectly named it was, considering that these modern-day buccaneers had made it their base in Cruz Bay. Poor Esteban—he'd walked right into the Buccaneer's Lair, not knowing it really *was* one!

Then I thought about Jenna. How could she have worked there the whole time, side by side with that bartender, seeing the kinds of people he hung out with, and not realizing the danger she was in?

Or maybe she *had* realized—maybe that was why she'd been so terrified. Maybe that's why she'd been kidnapped and brought here tonight.

Innocent until proven guilty . . .

Joe and I didn't say a word to each other as we spied on the gang of pirate-kidnappers. We didn't make a sound. Our lives, and perhaps the lives of two other people, depended on our total silence.

I tried to make sense in my mind of what I was seeing, and of what I had seen earlier back on the road. Somehow the gang must have figured out that Joe and I were still on the island.

How had they known? Had there been someone on the boat with us, just to make sure we arrived on St. Thomas?

There must have been. With so much at stake, a gang this size would not have taken any chances.

Out of the ruins now stepped the hulking figure of Cap'n—Mr. Corbin St. Clare himself. Beside him walked the bartender from the Buccaneer's Lair, carrying the ransom money in its metal briefcase. He placed it down on a flat stump, snapped it open, and the two of them started counting the loot.

Joe motioned me away from the scene. I knew what he meant—we needed to talk, but we were too close to make noise. We backed away down the trail about a hundred feet, just far enough to whisper.

"We've got to find Esteban," he said. "He has to be around here somewhere."

"And Jenna, too," I reminded him.

"I say we circle the campsite in different directions and meet up on the far side, down by the beach," he said.

"And if one of us finds them?"

"He waits for the other to show up before he does anything."

"Excellent. Let's do it."

Joe and I set off into the forest, he to the right of the trail, me to the left. Luckily, there wasn't much underbrush—just palm trees and spiny bushes rooted in sand and dried seaweed from past storms. It was pretty easy to make headway without making any noise that would alert the gang to our presence.

My route took me behind the ruins of the sugar mill, heading toward the beach. In between the two, there was a clearing with two lean-tos—shelters made of palm leaves and branches, propped on bamboo poles. Even with the full moon rising, it was dark under the canopy of the trees. But the glow of the bonfire showed me their shapes.

I crept close to the nearer, larger lean-to and inched along its side so that I could peek inside through the open front.

Just as I got into position, I heard a voice inside the lean-to that made me freeze in place.

"Hello, baby—how're you doing?"

Jenna!

For a second, I thought she was talking to me—that's how close her voice was. I nearly answered her too—but someone else did first.

"I'm all right," a man's voice replied. It was a voice I hadn't heard before, with just a faint hint of an accent. "I could use a drink. . . ."

"I'll get you some water," Jenna said. Then she walked out of the lean-to—right past me. I mean *right past*, not two feet away! She didn't see me, though, because I was in the dark shadow cast by the lean-to's wall.

What was going on here?

Jenna wasn't handcuffed. She didn't even seem scared anymore—not the way she'd looked sitting next to the driver of the car that tried to run us down.

I watched as she disappeared around the side of the ruins, headed for the bonfire.

I had to know who she was getting water for! She'd called him "baby." Was he her boyfriend?

At that moment I felt a hand on my shoulder, and I nearly jumped out of my skin.

"Joe!" I whispered.

He put a finger up to his lips to shush me. I responded by pointing at the lean-to, letting him know there was someone inside. He seemed to get it.

There was no discussion of what to do next. We had to take the chance that we could overcome whoever was in there. After all, it was just one person, and he was sick, supposedly.

But could we take him down before he shouted for help?

We had to bet that we could. If we succeeded, when Jenna came back, we could take her away from here, out of danger. Then we could try to find Esteban.

I lifted one finger, then another, and another. One, two, three—GO!

We ran into the lean-to and tackled the reclining figure lying on a blanket inside. I put my hand on his mouth to stop him from crying out.

Then I got a good look at his face. It was filthy—obviously, he hadn't washed in days—but I recognized him anyway.

"Esteban!" I whispered. "Joe, it's him!"

The face was the same as in the photograph, except he was now in a state of shock. His brow was clammy—it was obvious he had some kind of fever—and his eyes stared up at me and Joe in sheer terror.

"It's okay," Joe whispered to him. "We're here to help you."

"Your father sent us," I explained. "We're going to get you and Jenna out of here, then get the police to come round up these dirtbags."

His eyes shifted left, then right, then he looked back up at us and nodded his head to show he understood.

"Quiet, now," I said. "Don't make a sound."

I lifted my hand off his mouth, and he tried to sit up, resting himself on one elbow. I gave him a little help.

The whole time, though, I was thinking a mile a minute. Something was weird about all this. Why had Jenna called him "baby"? And why had the gang let its two prisoners be alone together, unguarded and free to escape?

"Baby? I'm back."

Jenna stepped inside the tent, carrying a hacked-open coconut filled with water. Seeing me and Joe, she nearly dropped it.

"Shhh!" I said, a finger to my lips. "We're getting you out of here, right now!"

She looked at Esteban, and then they both looked at us.

Clearly, they hadn't been expecting us. As far as Jenna was concerned, we'd been run off a cliff, so I could understand why she looked like she'd seen a ghost.

Still, you'd have thought they'd both be happy to see us.

Instead, Esteban's face grew hard and cold. "Help!" he cried out all of a sudden. "In here! Intruders!"

His voice rang out in the quiet of the ruins, where all had been quiet and muffled before. Suddenly, the whole place broke into commotion. Everyone started yelling and running, and in a moment, Joe and I were surrounded.

We stood there like a couple of dummies, totally shocked and stupefied.

Meanwhile, Jenna helped Esteban to his feet. "You okay, sweetheart?" she asked him.

"Jenna!" I said, my jaw hanging slack with surprise. "You . . . and him . . . ?"

She shrugged. "Sorry, Frank," she said. "I was just doing my job."

"You mean, getting me out of my room so it could be searched?" I said bitterly.

I realized now that I'd been tricked—made stupid by Jenna's good looks. I'd allowed her to lead me by the nose, and the whole time, she'd been spying on our activities for the gang!

Just then, Corbin St. Clare came into the lean-to.

He walked up to Esteban and threw a friendly arm around his shoulder. "How ya feelin', boss?" he asked.

Boss?

Esteban Calderon was the boss of the bounty hunters who were supposed to have kidnapped him?

It all began to come clear now. "I thought you said they were dead," Esteban said to Cap'n.

"I ran 'em down, that's all I can tell ya," Cap'n replied with a shrug. "Like I said the last time, they're hard to kill. Anyway, they'll be dead soon enough. Third time's the charm."

He laughed, looked at us with an evil smile, and said, "We'll just have to make real sure you boys die this time."

11.

The Worm Turns

"Tie 'em up," Cap'n instructed his men.

Frank and I were wrestled to the ground and our hands tied behind our backs. Then we were placed back-to-back and tied together.

"You two stay here while we get packed up," Cap'n told us—like we could have gone somewhere if we wanted to. "Keep an eye on 'em, Jenna." Then he walked away, followed by his men.

Esteban went over to Jenna and kissed her—a long kiss, right in front of us. Then, turning to Frank, he smiled—a really mean, nasty smile that turned his handsome face ugly—and left the lean-to.

"Jenna," Frank said, ignoring Esteban, "how can you let them kill us? You've got to help us get loose!"

She stared at the floor, unable to look either of us in the eye.

"What are you doing with this bunch of cutthroats anyway?" Frank went on. "You're not like them, I can tell. Help us, Jenna! Quickly!"

She looked up at him with those huge, sad, green eyes of hers, and said, "Sorry, Frank. I meant it when I said you're really sweet. And I didn't know they were going to try to kill you. But it's too late now. If I help you and your brother, I'll either wind up in jail, or dead."

"It's not too late!" Frank begged her. "Please! Think of how our parents will feel when they get the news. If you let them kill us, we'll never get to live our lives . . . have families . . . children . . ."

I knew Frank was working on her, trying to make her feel guilty so she'd help us. If you ask me, though, he was laying it on a little thick.

I mean, I could see she was beginning to soften, but she was still far from wavering, let alone cracking. And who knows how soon the others would return and make an end of Frank and me.

"I told you, it's too late for you. I've messed up royally, but it can still work out for me. Esteban says we're leaving this island tonight—for good."

"And where will you go?" Frank asked her.

Me, I kept my mouth shut. I figured Frank had a

better chance of getting to her, knowing their history together.

"Esteban's the son of a famous man," he said, "a man who can send people like me and my brother halfway around the world to find his son. Do you think, if you let them kill us, we'll be the last to come looking for him?"

She was looking at the floor again. He'd gotten to her with that one, nicked her good.

"But Esteban's my ticket to the big time."

"Are you kidding?" I broke in. "A girl like you, with your looks, could get a big modeling contract! You could be an actress in the movies! What do you need with a skeeve like that?"

She smiled at me out of one corner of her mouth. "I actually did try acting for a while," she said. "They told me I was pretty good at it."

"You sure fooled me," Frank said bitterly.

She sighed. "But I didn't like Hollywood, and the way people treated me. Esteban knows how to treat a girl like royalty. When we get to the Riviera, he's going to drape me in jewels from head to toe. That's what he told me."

"He's a liar!" I said, trying hard not to speak above a whisper—which was hard, because I really wanted to scream at her. "Why do you believe him? He's lied to everybody from day one!"

"Not to me," she said. "He's never lied to me. I've known about this whole plan from the word go. Plundering the wreck, the fake kidnapping, everything."

Frank sighed. "Sorry, Joe. I let you down. I should have known not to trust anyone."

"No worries, bro," I told him. "We'll get out of this somehow."

"Don't count on it," Jenna said.

By this time I was getting frantic. I kept looking around, trying to find something—anything—that would help us get out of this. Soon the gang would come back. Frank and I had only a few minutes to convince this girl to change her mind.

But how?

"Tell me," Frank said to her, "if we're going to die, I'd like to know the whole story. Whose idea was this whole scheme?"

"It was Esteban's," she said, with a hint of pride. "He was down here when the wreck was discovered. We were already an item, although we weren't going out much, because I had to work. He promised me I'd never have to work again, if he could bring this off."

"How come you're leaving tonight, then?" I

asked. "There's still a lot of treasure down there, waiting to be stolen."

"It got too hot, with the coast guard and the park rangers and whatnot. We'd only gotten halfway through, but Esteban could see right away it was too much trouble. That's when he got the idea to get his father's money now, instead of having to wait till after the old man died."

This Esteban guy was really pond scum, if you asked me. Just because his dad happened to be a big-time diplomat didn't excuse the son's being a total pig.

I didn't like the way he'd rubbed it in with Frank, either. Nobody beats on my big brother in front of me and gets away with it.

"Jenna," Frank pleaded in a whisper, "please! You didn't know they'd try to kill us. You can testify against the rest of the gang and get off with just a slap on the wrist! Joe and I will speak for you, and—"

"Stop," she said, her chin trembling now. "I can't. I told you already, I just can't."

Just then, we heard the footsteps of the gang approaching. Tears streaming from her eyes, Jenna leaned forward, took Frank's face in her hands, and whispered, "Good-bye."

She was still eye-to-eye with him when Esteban appeared, holding up a heavy, old-fashioned metal lantern with a curved glass shade. His eyes flashed darkly in the lantern's light. He strode forward, grabbing Jenna and yanking her away from Frank.

"What do you think you're doing?" he yelled at her, shoving her away so hard she crumpled to the ground with a harsh cry of pain.

Esteban turned back to Frank, murder in his eyes. "Why . . . don't . . . you . . . die!?" he screamed, swinging the lantern full-force right at Frank's head. Its metal base hit him square in the side of the head with a sharp, sickening crunch.

The glass shattered, and I had to duck and wince as I felt the shards whiz by my face.

My heart was racing now in panic. Every shred of my being wanted to protect Frank, to smash Esteban, and to get us out of here alive.

But there was nothing I could do. Even the single-edged razor blade I kept near the front of my belt would do me no good at this point, because the thugs were already attaching leg irons to my ankles.

Welded to the leg irons was a heavy iron chain, and on the other end of the chain, an iron ball that must have weighed a hundred pounds.

"We found these old things at the wreck site," Cap'n said, pleased with himself. "I thought we'd keep 'em for souvenirs. Ye never know when a ball and chain'll come in handy. Like when someone's goin' to walk the plank!"

And with that, he let out a hideous howl of laughter. The gang all joined in, and soon the entire campsite echoed with the sound.

Meanwhile, I could see the blood matting Frank's hair. He was out cold, and there wasn't a thing I could do to help him.

I stared over at Jenna, wordlessly begging her to help us.

She was still lying on the floor, propped on one elbow and clearly shell-shocked. I guess being brutalized by your boyfriend is a real wake-up call. The blood on Frank's head had its effect too. It made our case better than Frank had managed to do with all his words.

But it was too late. Jenna couldn't help us now, even if she'd wanted to.

"Haul 'em aboard," Cap'n bellowed. "The boss and I will take care of 'em, and then come back for the rest of ya."

"You're going to 'take care' of us?" I asked. "How exactly are you planning to do that?"

Cap'n smiled his gold-toothed grin at me. "Oh, I think we'll introduce ya to Davy Jones's locker. They say the sea bottom is chock full of interesting species never seen by man. I guess you'll find out soon enough."

12.
Walking the Plank

I woke up with a crashing headache. The ground was moving up and down, making me nauseous. Then I realized—it wasn't my imagination. We really *were* going up and down. We were on a boat.

I was sitting, my back leaning against the side of the boat. Joe was next to me on my left. Both our hands were tied, but in front of us, not behind like before—and at least we weren't still attached to each other.

The boat's engine was roaring. Obviously, we were going full speed ahead. Looking back to my right, I saw the bonfire at the sugar mill ruins getting smaller and smaller. Behind it, the dark bulk of the island with its central mountains loomed blacker than the sky, which was full of stars and lit by a full moon.

Not that I could appreciate the beauty of the scenery. My head was totally splitting. I knew I'd been hit with something, but I couldn't remember with what or by whom. All I knew was that the side of my head was caked with blood—I could still feel a drop or two trickling down my ear, but for the most part, the bleeding seemed to have stopped.

"You okay?" Joe asked me.

I nodded yes. I could only hear him because he was shouting in my ear. Jenna, Esteban, and Cap'n were up front by the wheel, and couldn't hear a word—not that it mattered.

Every few seconds Jenna glanced back at us, then looked away before Esteban caught her doing it. She seemed troubled, which I was glad about. It meant she at least had a conscience buried somewhere inside that head of hers.

I'd tried my best to get her sympathy so she'd help us get free—but it had been no use. Well, I guess it had made her think twice about Esteban, anyway—because now, every time he tried to put his arm around her, she sort of shied away from him.

I could tell he was annoyed by that too—he kept looking from her, to me, and back to her again, with a horrible scowl on his face.

Though my head was pounding something fierce, I wasn't totally out of it. I was aware enough to notice that in his left hand, Esteban clutched the handle of the briefcase holding the ransom money.

It was easy to figure out why he hadn't left it behind. He didn't trust the gang members with it, and who could blame him? As they say, "There's no honor among thieves."

After a while, Cap'n cut the motor, and we started to drift, bobbing up and down in the swells of the open ocean. He turned to face us and wiped his hands on his shirt.

"Well, now," he said, smiling his gold-toothed smile. "We've passed the twelve-mile limit. That means we're out of reach of the laws of the USA."

He didn't have to explain what that meant. He'd taken us out here to throw us overboard where no one would ever find us. Even if he was caught, it would be much harder to convict him of a crime committed in international waters.

"Time to get rid of the excess baggage," Cap'n said. "Right, boss?"

"Right," Esteban said.

"Hey," Joe said suddenly, looking at Esteban. "How come he calls you boss, but he gives all the orders?"

"Shut up," Cap'n said, scowling at Joe. He picked up a baseball bat that was lying on the deck and raised it over his head threateningly.

Esteban put out a hand. "Calm yourself," he told Cap'n. "There's no need for blood."

"You're a fine one to say that," Cap'n shot back, "after what you did to the other kid's head."

Esteban turned a steely gaze on him. "When I want your opinion, I'll tell you what to say."

"Is that right?" Cap'n said, tightening his grip on the baseball bat. "Look, sonny, you may have had the original idea, but me and my boys have got the treasure now. Give me one reason why we shouldn't ditch you—and your girlfriend, too?"

All of a sudden, he swung the bat at Esteban, catching him in the upper left arm.

Esteban cried out in pain, dropping the briefcase onto the deck. Cap'n tried to reach down and get it, but Esteban gave him a swift kick in the face, sending him reeling backward. Before Cap'n could recover, Esteban had pulled a pistol out of his pocket and was pointing it at him.

"How's this for a reason?" he asked, waving the gun. "You should have broken my right arm, you thug."

"Go ahead, shoot me," Cap'n told him. "What

do you think my boys will do to ye when ye get back to shore and they find out I'm not with ye?"

Cap'n was crouched down low. From where I sat, I could see that he was grabbing something on the deck behind him. Suddenly, he threw it at Esteban, leaping at him at the same moment.

Esteban's hands flew up to block the diving mask that was headed straight for his face. His gun went off, but it was pointing straight up in the air.

He never got off a second shot. Cap'n was on him, pummeling Esteban with his right hand while pinning his pistol hand with his left.

Jenna, meanwhile, was screaming her head off. "No! No! Stop it!" she cried.

But Cap'n didn't stop. Not till Esteban lay still, his nose bloodied. The gun was limp in his hand. Cap'n took it from him, and the man he'd called "boss" did not resist.

Jenna backed away in horror, her hand covering her mouth, as Cap'n rose and pointed the gun right between her eyes.

"Okay, missy. Enough foolin' around. Time to get down to business. I'm in charge now."

Jenna's hand went to her throat. I saw the sheer panic in her eyes as they darted left and right, looking for a way out.

"Now help me toss these boys overboard."

"Jenna, no!" I yelled.

She looked at me—stared right at my head, where her boyfriend Esteban had clocked me. And she froze.

"Do it!" Cap'n roared. I could see the whites of his eyes as he pointed the gun—a truly frightening sight.

Then he waved the gun at Esteban. "Do it now, or I'll blow your boyfriend's brains out!"

Jenna slowly walked over to me. I let her help me up to a standing position. We stood close to each other—facing each other—and her frightened green eyes looked straight into mine.

What do I do? I knew she was silently asking me.

I had no answer.

"Do it now!" Cap'n bellowed, even louder this time. He fired a shot in the air.

Jenna screamed, then turned back to me, her hands trembling. But I saw in her eyes that she'd thought of something. They didn't look panicked anymore—just terribly, terribly sad.

She took my bound hands in hers and squeezed. I felt her hand put something in mine—a hard object whose shape I recognized.

Then she kissed me softly on the cheek and said, "Good-bye, Frank. I'm so sorry."

She bent down and pushed the heavy cast iron

ball that was chained to my feet. She rolled it toward the gap in the railing where Cap'n was standing. I had no choice but to shuffle along behind it, or it would have yanked me from my feet—that's how heavy it was.

"Wait!" I heard Joe yell from behind me.

I turned to look. Somehow he'd gotten to his feet on his own. "Me first."

"No, Joe!" I said. "I'm the oldest."

He stared hard at me, and, in the semidarkness of the full moon, I thought I saw him wink, just slightly. It was more like a twitch—but I knew Joe, and they didn't. I was sure he was trying to tell me something.

"You may be the oldest, but I'm the strongest."

"Ha!" Cap'n laughed. "Not strong enough to get free of that ball and chain." He walked over to Joe. "But I like your spunk, mate. You'd have made a good partner in crime. Too bad you're honest."

He took Joe by the elbow and led him forward, past me and Jenna, over to the gap in the railing. "Well, I'm going to grant you your wish, my friend. You get to go first."

I can't tell you how I felt at that moment. I was barely in my own right mind. My brother was about to be murdered right in front of my eyes—and I was totally helpless to stop it!

Joe stood at the edge of the deck and looked right at Jenna. "He's going to kill Esteban next, and you, too—don't think he won't."

"Don't listen to him," Cap'n said. "Once we get rid of these two, you and me are heading back to pick up the others." He pointed to Esteban. "We'll dump this one, load up the gang and the loot, and head straight for the Bahamas. I've got a private island waiting for us there, where we can divvy up the treasure. After that, each can go his own way."

"He's lying to you," Joe said, staring intently at Jenna. "Why should he keep you around and give you a share of the loot? You see how easily he kills people."

"All right, that's enough out of you," Cap'n said. He gave Joe a hard sock in the gut. Joe doubled over.

"Now pick up that ball," Cap'n ordered him, "before I hit you again."

Joe picked up the heavy iron ball—not an easy trick when your hands are tied together. As he stood up, he gasped, "Jenna . . ."

Jenna knew he was pleading with her to do something. But she was not about to take on a bad guy with a gun, and Joe knew it.

What he didn't know, and I did, was that Jenna had already done something to help.

She'd handed me the key.

"Wait!" I said, bending down and picking up the iron ball I was attached to. "We'll jump together."

"Ah, the perfect solution!" Cap'n said with a smile that was way too cheerful. I could see he was really enjoying this, the sicko.

"All right, step away now, girlie," Cap'n told Jenna. He pointed to the gap in the railing and said, "Now—jump!"

"Good-bye, Joe," I said, choking up a little. "You . . . you were the best brother ever."

Joe's eyes were welling up too. Neither of us was giving up yet, but we both knew this could be it—these could be the last words we ever said to each other.

It was hard to take.

"One," I said.

"Two," Joe said.

"Three!" we both shouted.

Taking a last, deep breath, we leaped side by side into the black water.

JOE

13.
The Deep

We sank like a pair of stones. I tried not to panic, but it was impossible.

Thankfully, the bottom here wasn't very deep—maybe thirty feet. I could still see the full moon through the clear water, though dimly.

Frank and I hit the bottom side by side. Instantly, I started digging into my belt with my fingers, feeling for the single-edged razor I always keep there. If I could get both our hands free, maybe we'd have a chance to live through this, although I couldn't think how.

That's what Frank is best at—getting great ideas just when we need them most. And I knew he had something up his sleeve. I could tell.

I got the razor out and slashed through the plastic cuffs that bound my wrists together. Precious seconds went by as I went to work on Frank's.

This was why it had been so important for us to jump together. Frank knew I had the razor. And if the boat had drifted between his jump and mine, I'd never have gotten close enough to free him.

I cut through Frank's bonds. Then, just as I was thinking, *Now what?* Frank held up what looked like a key! What little light was left caught it.

It was the old-fashioned skeleton-type key—you know the kind. This one looked really old. I sure hoped it wouldn't break when Frank tried it on our leg irons.

He unlocked himself, but it took a good long while. When you're holding your breath, five seconds seems like an hour. Finally, he stepped out of his irons and got busy on mine.

By the time he got me free, I felt like my lungs were about to burst. I willed myself not to pass out. If I did, I knew there was no way I'd survive.

We swam for the surface. It seemed impossibly far away.

Both Frank and I can hold our breath for a really long time—more than two minutes—but it's different when you're in a swimming pool having fun, trying to see who can hold his breath longer.

When your heart is racing in panic, it uses up more oxygen and puts out more carbon dioxide—the stuff that makes you pass out if you don't exhale.

On the other hand, once you do exhale underwater, you have only a few seconds before you pass out from lack of oxygen. In a swimming pool, you can surface in less than a second. But here?

Luckily, the surface looked farther away than it really was. The moon still seemed dim and far away when we broke through, gulping and gasping for air.

It took a good while before either Frank or I had recovered enough to speak. By that time, though, we'd both looked around and had seen that the boat was nowhere in sight.

For the second time in less than twenty-four hours, we'd been abandoned at sea—only this time, we were twelve miles from shore, much farther than the last time. There would be no life-saving buoys to hang onto out here.

We were on our own.

We could see the lights of St. Thomas in the distance. I knew it couldn't be St. John, because there were just too many lights. The current had to be taking us westward. "Hey, Frank," I said. "If we keep drifting, we'll wind up in Puerto Rico."

"Great," he said sarcastically. "Like we'd ever get that far."

"Why not?" I asked, as we floated on our backs to save precious energy.

"Remember what happened at the wreck site?" he said.

"You mean those sharks?"

"Mm-hmm."

"Well, maybe they sleep at night."

"Sharks don't sleep, Joe. They have to keep moving all the time or they can't breathe. It's how they're built."

"Well, then, how do they rest?"

"With one eye open."

"Well . . . then maybe they rest with one eye open at night."

"Let's hope so," he said.

We tried swimming toward the lights, but they were impossibly far. We alternated periods of floating, recovering our energy, then swimming some more. But at this rate, we'd be past the island by the time we got anywhere close to shore.

The sky began to lighten, and the lights on shore

started going out. I was beyond exhausted, and I knew Frank had to be too. Somehow, though, we kept going. Neither of us wanted to die like this—not after escaping death so many times in just the past two days.

The first shark fin appeared just as the sun was about to break over the eastern horizon. "Uh-oh," I said. "Frank? Don't look now, but—"

"I see it, bro," he said. "Just stay cool. Don't move."

We floated on our backs some more. The fin kept circling us, and soon it was joined by three more.

"Here we go again," I said.

Just then, though, we heard the sound of a boat's motor.

"HELP! HELP!" we both yelled at the top of our lungs. We waved our arms frantically in the direction of the noise. We couldn't see the boat, because we were staring right into the rising sun—but that meant whoever was on the boat would have a better view of us.

Unfortunately, so did the sharks. They started coming in closer to check us out. I could see that the blood had soaked out of Frank's hair and into the water—and you know how sharks get when they smell blood.

They get *excited*. And when you're waving your arms and yelling like a maniac, it gets them even *more* excited.

"*Ow!*" I heard Frank yell.

"What?" I shouted. "Did you get bit?"

"Yes—no, not bit, stung."

"Stung?"

All of a sudden, I felt a searing, burning pain on my back. "YEOW!"

It wasn't sharks, though. It was a school of jelly-fish, and we'd drifted right into their path. Every few seconds, Frank or I would brush across one of their toxic tentacles and feel the shock of another sting.

On the other hand, the sharks seemed to be keeping their distance. I guess they didn't want to get stung themselves.

The noise of the boat's motor got louder, and now we could see it—a black silhouette blocking the sun. It was a fishing boat. I could see the nets strung out along its sides. It pulled up alongside us—and then I heard gunshots!

Were they trying to kill us? Was it the *Leaky Sieve*, coming back to finish us off?

"Ahoy, down there!" a voice bellowed. "We'll throw you a line!"

Now I understood—the gunshots were to scare away the sharks. Looking over my shoulder as we swam for the line, I couldn't spot the circling fins any longer.

A few minutes later we were lying on the deck of the fishing boat *Happy Daze*, heading back toward Cruz Bay.

Zuzu Johnson, the fisherman who'd rescued us, radioed ahead for medical help. We were going to need it—both Frank and I had jellyfish stings all over our bodies, and we were beginning to swell up something awful. Frank's wound was going to need a few stitches, too.

"Dude," I said to Frank, "you look really messed up."

"Me? You are the ugliest thing I've ever laid eyes on."

"Me? No, you."

"No, you."

"No, you."

Hey, at least we knew we were still alive.

Captain Rollins of the National Park Service was there at the dock to meet us, along with the ambulance that would take us to Cruz Bay's local community clinic.

We filled him in on what had happened, and he

promised to alert the police and the FBI. Hopefully, Cap'n and his gang were still down at Reef Bay, loading up the *Leaky Sieve* with their treasure. They would be in a hurry, but there was an awful lot of treasure to stow aboard.

The ambulance took us to the clinic, where they gave us antivenom and antihistamines to keep us from swelling up so much we'd explode.

As we lay there in our hospital beds, the pain of the stings shooting darts through our bodies, we heard the roar of what had to be an entire fleet of police helicopters overhead.

"They're on their way," Frank said, managing a smile.

"Sounds like it," I agreed.

"I hope they're in time."

"They will be," I assured him.

It had been several hours since we'd walked the plank, but what with loading up the boat, and making sure nothing was left behind at the dark campsite by the ruins, the *Leaky Sieve* would surely still be in U.S. waters, even if she had shoved off.

"I just hope he didn't kill Jenna," Frank said.

"I don't think he would have," I told him. "Did you see the way he was looking at her?"

"What do you mean?"

"I think he was hoping to make her his girlfriend, once Esteban was out of the picture."

"You think so?"

"Uh-huh."

"But what about Esteban?"

I wasn't so sure about him. At that point, he might have been shark food, or they might just have left him behind on the beach in exchange for the ransom money.

One thing was for sure—now that the police were hot on their trail, Corbin St. Clare's gang of thieves and kidnappers would soon be rounded up.

The doctor came in to examine us. "You boys feeling better now?" she asked.

"Much better, thanks," I said.

"Me too," Frank agreed.

"We're going to keep you here for the rest of today, then let you go tomorrow if you're well enough."

"Hey, Frank," I said, "that still leaves us with four days here before we have to go home."

"Oh, no," he said. "No way I'm hanging around this place. It may be paradise, but it's way too dangerous for my taste."

"Totally," I said. "After this 'vacation,' I'm going to need a vacation."

"Me too," Frank said. "Only this time, let's stay home in the snow and cold."

"I hear you, bro," I said. "I hear you."